TOUGH TO TENDER

TOUGH TO TENDER

MARY ANN KENNEDY

iUniverse, Inc.
New York   Bloomington

TOUGH TO TENDER

iUniverse books may be ordered through booksellers or by contacting:

iUniverse
1663 Liberty Drive
Bloomington, IN 47403
www.iuniverse.com
1-800-Authors (1-800-288-4677)

ISBN: 978-1-4502-2746-9 (sc)
ISBN: 978-1-4502-2747-6 (ebk)

Printed in the United States of America

iUniverse rev. date: 04/14/2010

I would like to dedicate this book to the following:
Lisa, Merle, Scerrell, Teresa, (Joe) Larry, Jim and my grandson Hunter.

CONTENTS

THE BEGINNING
CHAPTER 1

The city of Atlanta, Georgia has many secrets and also the charm of the good old south. However, the story that you are about to read, will give you a new and terrifying feeling, of what could and does go on in our loving southern people. The news of this story will shock you, to your core.

Earl Ralph Chamberlain was a very handsome thirty-two year old man with a kind and gentle soul, who lived on a plantation in Atlanta, Georgia. The large three stories Historical home, was filled with unique antique furniture and southern comfort. It was nestled against the trees in the formal garden, with a garden centerpiece being a large fountain.

In the fountain's center were lovebirds at the top, with water always flowing evenly down into it, filled with Koki-fish jumping through the water, as though they were playing leap frog. Spread throughout the garden, were stepping stone walkways, each stone engraved with a special memory, photo and date, imitating the hand made quilts of Georgia.

On the right side of the garden were colorful flowers, some heavily blooming along the garden fence. As you walk on the trail, reading each stone and looking around at all the beautiful color, it was as though you were in a wonderful world of your own. On the left of the garden, was an old Victorian style gazebo, that had handing baskets of different vines, with colorful leaves, almost reaching the floor, wicker furniture to sit back and take it all into your soul.

Ralph lived a peaceful life although he was lonely, because his parents had died. He had consumed his life, with his work, trying not to think about the loneliness he felt. He could have lived out his life traveling the world, just taking life easy, after all his parents had left him a wealthy man. However, he did not do that; instead he was the founder and sole owner of The Chamberlain Computer Company.

He was well known in the city, even in the state for generously giving to various charities and entertaining politicians, with grand parties at his home, on the plantation. He was loved and respected by everyone that met him, for his wisdom and charm. Life could not be better for Ralph, nevertheless, he was still lonely and that is something that money can not buy, is love.

One day, as Ralph was busy in his large southern custom designed three story offices building, that made him feel at home, he received a call. A gentleman, by the name of Edward Scott, from Houston Texas, was on the phone, "Mr. Chamberlain, I hear that you are the man, I needed to call to help me with changing computers for my company. Could you fly out here for a business meeting to discuss this transaction?"

Ralph had employees in his company, that would normally have handled this matter; after all, he was the president of the company, but for some reason he wanted to go. "Yes, Mr. Scott, I will fly out for a meeting with you." He had a good feeling about it; he was unaware, that this meeting would change his life, forever and there is no turning back...

Only a week, later Ralph arrived at the airport in Houston, Texas and Mr. Scott's limousine driver was there to pick him up. Ralph was looking around at all the tall buildings, as they were going through the city. When they arrived at the Scott building, he was thinking "there is no warmth, in the building; it is strictly business." I wonder if that is how Mr. Scott will be, because he did not sound like that on the phone."

However, as Ralph was approaching the office of Mr. Scott, the door opened and there he stood. Ralph was shocked as he stared at this large man wearing a Stetson hat, rattle snake boots, a wide belt buckle with a bull in the center, and a black suit. Mr. Scott smiled and popped Ralph on the back of the shoulder, saying "Howdy, Sir, it is a pleasure meeting you in person and who is this with you?" as he was pointing to some chairs in his office, for them to be seated.

Ralph said, "Mr. Scott I would like to introduce you to my secretary, Mr. Kevin Wade" both of them were smiling at Mr. Scott, as they all shook hands. "Ha, Ha" laughed, Mr. Scott saying "Why, Sir, I have never known a male secretary before, because all secretaries I have known, are little fillies," as his body was still shaking from his laugher.

Ralph frowned, as he was roughly, saying, "Mr. Scott, I assure you that Mr. Wade, is well qualified, to do the job" Mr. Scott stopped his laughter, "I am sure he is; are you ready to get started with the meeting?" Ralph said, "Certainly." However, as the meeting was about to come to an end, the door flew open.

In walked, a very beautiful young lady. Ralph could not stop looking at her; she had long glowing blonde hair, olive complexion, a figure of a model and beautiful blue eyes. But, her mannerism was that of an arrogant snob, with no concern for anyone, but herself. She leaned down, lovingly kissed, Mr. Scott on the cheek, saying, "Hi Dad" then she sat down, for the remainder of the meeting.

Mr. Scott said, "Mr. Chamberlain, I would like you to meet my only child, Victoria Scott" Ralph shakes her hand, thinking, "She has the softest skin, I don't think, she has a fault anywhere, she is so beautiful." Then Mr. Scott turns to Mr. Wade "Victoria, this is Mr. Chamberlain's secretary, Mr. Wade."

With a soft sexy voice, she said, "It is a pleasure meeting you both," as she sits back down, pushing her long blonde hair behind her shoulders, to her back. Mr. Scott called his secretary in the room, saying, "Darlin' bring everyone a big glass of ice cold tea, please." Ralph was having a hard time concentrating, with Victoria in the room.

Ralph's heart was racing, as he was trying not to look at her, but somehow, he made it through the rest of the meeting. After the meeting had come to an end, he looked at Mr. Scott, asking, "Mr. Scott, would you mind, if I ask your daughter out, for a cup of tea?" He replied, "Why, Sir, my daughter is a grown woman, I suggest you ask her," as he, gave him, a pat on the shoulder, for the second time.

When he turned Victoria had already left the room, he rushed to the elevator to catch her before she left the building. He saw her standing, by the elevators and yelled, "Victoria, please wait for a moment!" As he approached her, he asks, "Victoria would you like to go out for lunch, with me?" she lingered, as she raised her left eye brow and said, "I will agree, provided it is at the country club."

Ralph sighed with relief, because he had fallen in love at the first sight of her; it did not matter how rude she was to him. At lunch he said to her, "Victoria you are the most beautiful woman, I have ever met" as his heart was skipping beats. Turning her head to the side, looking out of the corner of her eye, she replied, "Of course I am, why don't you tell me something, I don't already know."

The music was softly playing in the dining hall, Ralph looking at her seriously, as he asks, "Victoria, do you believe in love at first sight?" Softly pushing her long blonde hair back, looking straight at him, she harshly replied, "No, how ridiculous!" However, if you would like to call me later, I will accept your call."

Ralph smiled, "I will" He did not mind her attitude, because he knew it was that attitude that made her who she was. She said, "I hope you know what you are getting into." He smiled saying, "I do" after all he knew he did not have to take Victoria's attitude, because he was a good-looking, six-foot two-inches tall man, with black hair, built like a foot ball player, not to mention his wealth.

Nevertheless, Ralph pursued Victoria relentlessly, with phone calls, flowers, formal dinner parties, and extravagant gifts. Victoria loving it all, saying, "You know that you are spoiling me," as she wrapped her arms around his neck. Smiling, he replied, "No, you were already spoiled, I am just continuing what your father had already started."

Softly and sexy, she said, "Ralph, you know that if we continue to date, you will have to continue to spoil me." He replied, "Yes dear, I know" as he took her in his arms and kissed passionately. Ralph spent a month with Victoria in Houston, before returning to Atlanta, corresponding through the internet, overseeing his business.

After returning home, Mr. Scott accompanied Victoria to Atlanta to visit Ralph. He took Mr. Scott on a fox hunting trip and later they all three played golf. The time seemed to fly by, Mr. Scott and Ralph became very good friends and Victoria fell in love with Ralph, well as much as she was capable of loving.

The time was spent well between Mr. Scott and Ralph; fox hunting, fresh water fishing, golfing, and running their business, they learned how each other thought about things. Victoria was certainly spoiled, by both of them and life was looking good, for all of them. Before they knew it, a year had passed by and now Ralph wanted the relationship between him and Victoria to take the next step, marriage.

He flew to Houston for a surprise date, with Victoria. Ralph had called ahead and asks, "Victoria I wanted to take you out tonight, so could you dress formal" "Yes, but where are you taking me?" she asks. He said, "It is a surprise, just be ready alright, my love." She said, "Of course."

After he picked her up, she was surprised, when they arrived at the skylight room, for dinner and dancing. After they had eaten, Ralph took her hand, looked into her eyes and asks, "Victoria, will you give me the honor, of becoming my wife?" But, she turned to him, giving him a serious stare, as she said, "Under, one condition!"

Of course, Ralph looking puzzled asks, "And what condition is that, my love?" She replied, "You must promise me, that you will never say, the word No to me." His heart tighten in his chest, as he said, "I promise," as he felt that he may someday regret this decision, but he loved her more than his own life. Victoria thought a moment and answered, "Then my answer is yes!"

Victoria said, "Ralph you know that I am the social queen of Houston" as she was placing her hand, on her hip. Ralph replied, "Yes, and you now can be, the social queen of Atlanta." She said, "We have to have the wedding in Houston." Ralph said, "Love it takes so much time to plan a wedding, it would be more practical, if you moved in with me and planned it in Atlanta."

Victoria stated, "Ralph you know, I am saving myself for marriage" He said, "That is all right. My house is large enough and I won't pressure you." So Victoria agreed to move into Ralph's house to plan the wedding, and they set the date for June 12th. Victoria said, "I have to call my father," Ralph said, "Let's tell him in person tomorrow night, when we take him to dinner."

The next evening, they took Mr. Scott, to a steak restaurant for dinner. Ralph ordered champagne and Mr. Scott asks, "What is the special occasion?" Victoria said, "Well, Dad, Ralph has asked me to marry him and I said, yes." Mr. Scott smiled largely, as he hugged Victoria and shook Ralph's hand, saying, "Congratulations, I think you two are a prefect couple."

Ralph smiled, "Mr. Scott your daughter will be well cared for, because I love her with all of my heart." Victoria said, "Father we are flying to New York in the morning, to buy my engagement ring, from Tiffany's." Mr. Scott shouted, "Well let's toast to the future Bride and groom." It was a great night, they all enjoyed it.

The next morning, they flew to New York, and then took a cab to Tiffany's. Victoria was very picky, looking and looking, but Ralph was patient, because he knew this was the ring, that would be for a life time. After carefully looking, through each of the rings, she finally found it, a three carat, flawless, Lucida setting with clear brilliance.

Ralph took the ring, carefully placed it on Victoria's finger, as she hugged him saying, "I have never been so happy, Thank you."

Then they took separate planes home, Victoria, back to Houston and Ralph, back to Atlanta, because Ralph had to go back to work. Victoria called Ralph later and said, "If we have the wedding in Atlanta, then we have to have the reception in Houston, alright?" He said, "I agree, because everyone may not be able to come to Atlanta, at least they can come to the reception." She said, "Exactly."

Victoria called her friends to tell them, that her bridal registers, were Bloomingdale's and Tiffany's. One night, Victoria said to her father, "Father, don't get upset, but I am going to stay in Atlanta, at Ralph's house, while I am planning this wedding." He said, "I don't like that idea, but you are a grown woman, but I will ask, that you think it over well first."

Victoria called, Ralph and said, "I am coming to stay with you while I plan part of the wedding, but I need to reserve the skylight room, for the reception now." Ralph said, "Yes dear, I am looking forward to your coming here, come as soon as you can." Victoria's friends Elizabeth and Ann were excited and came over to her house to see the ring and help with the wedding plans.

Victoria said to them, "I am going to stay in Atlanta part of the time, to finish making my wedding plans" Elizabeth said, "You haven't slept with him, have you?" She shouted, "Of course not, you know I am saving my self for marriage." Elizabeth said, "Just checking, don't have a cow; we are your friends no matter, what."

Ann said, "We simply have to give you a bridal shower and a going away party, before you go." "Yes darling, you know we do" stated Elizabeth. Victoria said, "Yes, but let's have them together as one, because I have a lot of planning and organizing to do and I need your help." So they went to work, on the Bridal/going away shower/party.

The party was at the country club, with a live band. Ralph flew out for the party and to bring Victoria back with him. At the party Mr. Scott gave a toast then, gave Victoria an envelope. She opened it and saw two tickets for June 13th thru June 26th to the Greek Island for Thirasia; with a note saying, "I hope you two have a very happy life together and my gift to you two is this great honeymoon trip."

Of course, Victoria did not want to embarrass her father in front of anyone, so she hugged, him saying, "Thank-you," but whispered in his ear "I will speak to you later," with the voice of disapproval. She excused herself from the table and her friends followed her to the ladies room. Meanwhile, at the table Ralph asks, "Mr. Scott, I think this gift is a great gift, however, have you spoken to Victoria about this honeymoon, before now?"

Mr. Scott shouted, "Do you think I have gone crazy son? No, this was a surprise, besides Victoria will find something wrong about anything that we do." He continued, "Ralph you will learn the way to handle Victoria, is to announce a surprise like this in a group of people, then she will love it."

Then he said, "Ralph you are going to be my son-in-law, so why don't you call me Edward, instead of Mr. Scott." Ralph said, "Thank you, Edward and I just want you to know, I will take good care, of your daughter." Edward stated, "Ralph, you have made me a happy man, I hope you two have a great honeymoon."

The party was a great success, the guest count was about three hundred and the gifts were very nice, also. After the party, Ralph and Victoria flew to Ralph's home, in Atlanta. Victoria had sent several boxes of her belongings ahead, so she could have everything she needed, on her arrival. Ralph picked her up and carried her into the house, she angrily shouted "Ralph, put me down, this is not our honeymoon," so he gently put her down.

He said, "I know this is not our honeymoon, but I want you to feel comfortable in our home, you can decide which bedroom, you would like to stay in until the wedding." She turned and looked at him, saying, "Honey I am going to stay in the master bedroom, you choose another." Ralph smiled, "All right my love, I will move my things, now."

Victoria said, "I already feel at home and I have a lot to do before the wedding, so don't get in my way." Ralph said, "I would not think of it, my love, just let me know, if I can help" smiling, as he walked away. Victoria began to unpack, as Ralph was moving his things into one of the guest rooms.

Ralph began watching her, moving about the house rearranging things and thinking, she is the most beautiful woman I have ever seen and soon she will be my wife, how lucky can one man be to have everything? But, she was thinking, I can not wait to store all this old furniture and buy the modern furniture for my home.

A few days later, Victoria called Elizabeth and Ann, asking them to come to Atlanta to shop for her wedding dress. They were excited and came within the week. Victoria met them at the airport and on the way back home they stopped for breakfast. While they were eating, Victoria said, "I am so glad you two could come help me shop for my wedding dress."

Elizabeth said, "Victoria we have been friends since childhood, of course we wanted to come, this is exciting, I can't wait to get started." Ann said, "Me too, we are going to help you, find the most elegant dress." Victoria said, "Of course we are, After all, it is me we are talking about." They laughed and went to the plantation.

When they walked into the house, Elizabeth said, "Victoria, we know that the wedding reception will be at the skylight room in Houston, but where is the wedding to take place?" Ann said, "Yes, inquiring people want to know," laughing "Ha, Ha." She said, "Here at the plantation, I think it will make a beautiful outside wedding, just look at it what do you two think?"

Elizabeth said, "Oh Victoria you are right, this is a perfect place for an outside wedding." She shouted, "Ok, then the wedding will be here at the plantation;" "Now let's go shopping for my perfect wedding dress." So they all left for the shopping trip, laughing from excitement and joy. Victoria shouted, "This is going to be a great day."

Now here they are on Madison Avenue, walking into Bon Jon's Bridal Boutique in the middle of down town, Atlanta Georgia. Elizabeth looked around saying, "Oh my, there are so many to pick from" Ann said, "Victoria don't worry we will find the one for you." Victoria shouted, "There is only one for me, when I see it, I will know."

Bon Jon came out, introduced himself and had the girls to sit down for wine and cheese. He asks, "Now which one of you lovely girls are the bride to be?" Elizabeth pointed to, Victoria saying, "This is the bride to be, Can't you tell, she is simply beaming?" Bon Jon said, "Of course, now do you have any idea, what type of dress you are looking for."

Of course, Victoria was always strong-minded and to the point, she said, "Of course, I want an eloquent, some what, simple full skirted dress that will be great for a plantation outside wedding." Bon Jon said, "Great, now you girls sit back and enjoy your wine or champagne which ever you prefer, I will have the models come out shortly, with dresses that you will adore."

Soon the models were coming out, one at the time wearing, simply beautiful elegant dresses. Ann saw the third one, saying, "Oh Victoria this one is so beautiful, what do you think?" She frowned at her, saying, "I will know it, when I see it." After the twelfth model had come out, Bon Jon came out and asks, "Victoria have you see anything that you like?" She said, "Yes, but not, THE one."

So Bon Jon sent out the models again, wearing more dresses and when the twenty-first dress came out, Victoria shouted, "Stop! This is it." Bon Jon came out, smiling, "You have excellent taste, my dear" "Well of course I do," shouted, Victoria." Elizabeth and Ann said, "We agree with your choice, it is simply beautiful."

Bon Jon said, "Would you like to try it on now, my dear?" Victoria smiling, "Yes I would, thank you." Victoria tried it on and came out to show everyone, Bon Jon said, "My dear, you look like a princess" Elizabeth said, "Oh, Victoria, you are simply going to take everyone's breath away, when they see you at the wedding." Ann said, "I agree it is beautiful."

Victoria smiled, as she looked in the mirror at this beautiful white matte satin and Japanese fabric, with its strapless boned bodice, with embroidered and beaded, with the full skirt, having embroidered throughout its two layers and said, "I feel like a princess." Then Bon Jon brought out the matching gloves, that had the same embroider on them and Victoria smiled, as she put them on. Bon Jon said, "Now lasts but not least, the matching veil" as he placed it, on her head; it was beautiful white roses on the head piece and embroidery on the rest of the veil.

Elizabeth said, "Oh Victoria you are right, this is the perfect gown for you." Bon Jon stood gazing at her, she said, "Sir why are you staring at me" he said, "Please forgive me it is just that, I have never seen a more beautiful bride." Victoria asks, "Sir, Do you know a wedding planner, we can call for help with our wedding?"

Bon Jon replied, "My dear, that is my specialty" She said, "I did not realize that you were a wedding planner, too." After Victoria changed, back into her attire Bon Jon said, "Of course follow me" as he walked into another room, on the opposite side of the building. When they entered the room, he introduced them, to his secretary, "Victoria, Elizabeth, and Ann pointed to each girl, as he said their name, this is my secretary, and Joan she will gladly set up a time for us, to plan your wedding of the century."

Joan stood up and shook their hand asking, "Now which one of you ladies, is the bride to be?" while Joan was talking to them, Bon Jon left.

Victoria said, "I am the bride to be" pushing her long blonde hair back, as she always did. Joan asks, "What is the date of your wedding, dear and do you have a place that you, have in mind for the ceremony?"

Victoria stated, "My wedding will be June 12th and it will be on our plantation, outside." Joan said, "Oh my, we have to get started soon, if we only have six months of planning" "Yes, let's get started" said, Victoria. Joan said, "I see on the books that, Bon Jon can meet with you next, Thursday at 10:00 a.m., will that work with your schedule?" Victoria replied, "Yes" as she was checking, her date book, as well.

When Victoria and the girls got back to the plantation, they were exhausted from the day of shopping. Ralph was home and as they sat down for dinner, he asks, "Well, did you girls get anything accomplished, today?" Ann spoke up to say, "Oh yes, we," but before she could finish, Victoria said, "Yes, we found a wedding planner and we have to meet with him, next Thursday at 10:00 a.m.; I hope that will not be a problem for you, because I really want you to be there, but that's all, we did" looking at Elizabeth and Ann, urging them not to say anymore.

Later that night, as the girls were sitting in the hot tub, drinking tea, Elizabeth asks, "Victoria, why did you stop us from telling Ralph, about that beautiful wedding dress, we found today" She said, "Because I want to see the surprise on his face, when I walk toward him at the wedding." Ann said, "Oh, how romantic."

Elizabeth said, "I hate that we can't be here for the meeting, with Bon Jon Thursday However, we have to leave Tuesday." She said, "It will be all right, Ralph will be with me."

Next Thursday....... Ralph and Victoria walked into the boutique and Ralph said, "My love, this is a Bridal boutique" She said, "Be patient" then Bon Jon walked out and said, "This must be the groom, I heard about" smiling and shaking, his hand.

Bon Jon said, "Follow me" and they walked into a room filled with books, flowers and wedding accessories. Bon Jon asks, "Have you two decided on the color scheme?" "Yes we have, we want a total black and white wedding" said, Victoria. Ralph looked at Victoria with a surprise look on his face saying, "Black and White, you don't want color in the wedding?"

Bon Jon said, "I see, maybe you two would like a moment, to discuss this in private" "No, it is going to be the way she wants it, regardless of my opinion, so do what ever she wants" Victoria replied, "Yes, that is right" looking ever so serious, at Bon Jon. So Bon Jon never asks Ralph's opinion, again.

They had an engagement photo made for the newspaper, Ralph in a black suit with a red tie and Victoria in a beautiful red dress, the dress top was off the shoulders and full skirted. One announcement was placed in the Houston paper and the other in the Atlanta paper. The invitations were sent out. They were white with black writing and a black ribbon and the envelope was black with a white ribbon and white writing.

The Wedding..

The Plantation was set up with a terrace arch-way, for the bride and groom to stand under, to be married. It was filled with white roses through out. Two large water fountains, with love birds in the center, were placed one on each side of the yard. The chairs, with black chair covers and a ribbon tied in a bow were placed in between the two fountains.

The chairs were placed in two sections, with a white runway in the middle of the chairs, from the back of the chairs, to the terrace in the front. Large beautiful black flower pots were placed throughout the yard, filled with white flowers and a black and white ribbon, on each pot. There were large black and white ribbons, tied to trees round about the yard.

Finally, the music began to play, as Ralph is standing in front, awaiting his bride and the wedding, is about to begin. The bridesmaids are walking down the runway, with their beautiful simple black bridesmaids dresses, carrying a single white rose, with a black ribbon hanging down from it. Then here comes, Victoria holding on to her father's arm. Ralph looks at her, smiling as his heart, is racing, as he is thinking, "she is breath taking."

Victoria walks down in her beautiful wedding gown, holding her bridal bouquet of black and white roses, with white ribbons hanging down from it. Her father, whispers softly, to her, "Victoria, you are so beautiful today, I love you" She looks up at him saying, "I love you, too, father." Then he puts her hand, into Ralph's hand and whispers, to him, "Take care of her" Ralph whispers back, "I will, forever" and they get married.

Afterward, they go to the wedding cake, it was most unusual, it was a black three foot tall, three layers cake, with white roses and white ribbon coming down from it, it was simply beautiful. Victoria gave Ralph a piece first and then he gently placed a piece in her mouth. Mr. Scott walked over to Victoria and said, "I think it is time, for our father….daughter dance. He took her hand and led her out to the dance floor while, everyone watched.

Afterward, everyone began to dance, Ralph gently took Victoria by the hand and they danced for a long while. Later, Mr. Scott was standing near her and he reaches into his pocket and brings out a ring, saying, "Victoria this ring was your mother's, it has yours' and her birthstone on it and it now belongs to you."

She kissed him on the cheek, "Thank-you, father" as he places it on her finger. Victoria walked over to Ralph and placed her hand in his, looks up at him and says, "I love you Ralph." Ralph whispered in her ear, "Do you realize this is the first time, you have said those words, to me" she replied, "Of course, but now I mean them so I can say them," he smiled at her and she smiled back.

Mr. Scott stood up, gave a toast and said, "I have already given my gift to the bride and groom; they are tickets for the Greek Island and they are leaving tomorrow." Everyone clapped their hands, Victoria stood up and hugged her father saying, "Thank you again, father I love you." By this time everyone began to leave, Ralph and Victoria rushed out the door, while the people were throwing bird seed, smiling while saying "good-bye to everyone."

The next morning, they arrived at the airport bags in hand and wearing casual wear excited, happy and holding hands. When they were seated on the plane, Ralph turned, looked at Victoria saying, "My love, you do realize the first time you said I love you was after, our wedding?" Victoria replied, "Yes, what of it" He asks, "Why?"

She shouted, "Because I really did not know, until that very moment." He whispered, "My love, this is one of the happiest days of my life" She replied, "Me too" the rest of the plane trip was a joy, for them both. When the plane landed in Greece, they had to then board a helicopter the rest of their journey, to the Greek Inland of Thirasia.

It was so remarkable, how beautiful the blue water of the Mediterranean Sea gleams in the sun light, looking from a short distance, up in the white clouds. When they landed, it was a surprise, how remote an island it was, just west of Santorine, with a Village population of only two hundred and sixty eight people, looking at it from the helicopter Victoria said, "I wonder why my father choose, this island?"

A tour guide was waiting for them to land and introduced himself, "I am Louie, are you Mr. and Mrs. Ralph Chamberlain" Ralph said, "Yes, it is a pleasure to meet you, Louie" then Louie asks them, "Would you like to rest awhile, before you begin your honeymoon tour?" Victoria said, "Yes, we are exhausted; please take us to the hotel."

They had to walk through a vineyard of capers and pass a monastery. Victoria asks, "Why are we walking?" Louie replied, "As you can see Mrs. Chamberlain, there is no where for a vehicle to go in between our vineyards and you will be staying in an Inn, on the other side." Victoria shouted, "We are staying in an Inn, not a hotel, do you know who we are, young man?"

Ralph took her hand to clam her down, she quickly shook his hand, from hers' Louie said, "Yes, Mrs. Chamberlain, I am aware of who you are and I promise you will like your accommodations, because the island people built all the buildings, rich in color and beautiful, so the whole island is a pleasant and peaceful place to stay, just look around you."

Ralph looked and everywhere was color, even in the plants, with the sea breeze blowing softly, on the island he said, "Look Victoria, it is so great, just look at everything" she said, "I will look later, I am too tried, to look now." Louie said, "We are here" They looked and saw the Manola Inn, it had red steps that went around leading to the second and third story, outside of the block building, which was very colorful blue, white, and red.

Later, after their rest, Ralph called the tour guide asking, "Louie, how do we order food to our room." Louie asks, "Mr. Chamberlain, would you like for me to bring you the best on our menu?" Ralph replied, "Certainly, thank-you." After awhile, Louie knocked on the door, Victoria opened it and Louie brought in the food.

Louie said, "The special dish of Married Fava, Mulberry Sweet for dessert and a bottle of wine on ice, with two glasses and two lit candles, for the newlyweds" where all on the table that was rolled inside their room. Louie excused himself and Ralph and Victoria sit down to eat, but were surprised how fresh and delicious everything tasted.

That evening, Ralph was holding Victoria, as they looked out the window of their room at the view. The sea was moving peacefully, with the sea breeze blowing on them. The village was surprisingly quiet, soft lights were on throughout the small village, but you could still see the colorful buildings.

The next morning, Louie brought up to the room, a bottle of champagne and flowers, with a card which read, "Have fun kids" signed "Dad." Then the guide said, "Please forgive me, for not telling you sooner, your father arranged for you to have a private yacht, so when you are ready I will take you to it." Victoria shouted with excitement, "Did you hear that Darling, father has arranged for us to have a private yacht."

Ralph said, "Louie, thank-you we would like to go out tomorrow, if possible" He replied, "My name and number, is on the table by the bed, you can call anytime" and left the room. Victoria and Ralph enjoyed their breakfast and then, they called Louie for a tour of the Island. They first toured the Inn, in which they where staying.

Then Louie said, "We have twenty-one monasteries, here on the island, we can tour Kimisis tis Theotokou monastery, it is beautiful," then they stopped at the Heliport, where they met some of the island people, then stopped, where the wine was made and had a wine testing, with some of the people that like to dance and laugh, so Ralph and Victoria danced for a while.

Then they stopped, where the chloro cheese was made, passing by homes of the island people, that were also colorful finally, Victoria said, "I am ready to go back to the Inn now, so Louie took them back. When they were in their room, they made love all night. The next morning, as Victoria began to awaken, she saw Ralph standing by the window enjoying the view; she walked over to him and put her arms around him.

He put his arms around her too, looked down into her eyes and smiled. He said, "I have ordered breakfast, let's eat." After breakfast he asks, "My love, what would you like to do first today." She said, "Let's call Louie and go out on the yacht." Ralph went to the phone and called for Louie to come take them out.

Once they arrived on the yacht, Louie showed them around, there was a swimming pool, with a bar near by, a sauna, Jacuzzi and a place to have a massage. They went swimming and afterward, Ralph said,

"My love, let's have lunch" so they did. They had been out for two days, when Ralph noticed one of the maids' running to Louie, shouting and crying in the native tongue.

Ralph could not understand the Greek language, so he asks, "Louie, what is going on?" Louie said, "Follow me, one of the workers has fallen into the sea" Ralph gashed, as he shouted, "What?" as they ran toward all the people, that had gathered together. Ralph looked over the side rail and said, "Oh my God!" as he saw one of the other men pulling a raft, swimming toward the man floating, on the top of the water.

People were crying and screaming, when Victoria walked over to Ralph saying, "Ralph, darling, what is going on?" He turned, to her with concern for the man in his voice and said, "It appears that one of the workers' was having chest pains, when he apparently fell overboard and there is a man trying to reach him now, to rescue him."

Ralph looked back and there were two more men that had jumped in the water to help with the rescue, tying a rope to the raft and shouting, "pull him up." However, by the time the man was pulled out of the water, he was already dead. Everyone was hysterical, Louie explained to Ralph, "Mr. Chamberlain, all these workers are next of kin and have been working together for years; we have to go back NOW."

Ralph said, "Of course we do" Victoria shouted, "No, we do not, this is not our problem and it is not, going to ruin our honeymoon!" Louie shouted angrily, "It is the law, anytime there is a death, on a boat or ship it has to be reported to the police, right away." Ralph looked at Victoria, as he shouted, "His family needs to know about this and we are going back, now."

The yacht was starting to turn and Victoria shouted, "Why can't he just be put in the freezer or something, until we are ready to go?" Ralph was angry, as he shouted, "Victoria, how can you be so cold hearted, this man has a family and now he is dead." Furiously, she shouted, "What is that to us" Ralph was devastated and angry, as he shouted, "The honeymoon is over and we are going home, that is final!"

When they arrived back at the Inn, Ralph made reservations for a helicopter to pick them up and they went home. Disillusioned and bewildered by Victoria's actions Ralph realized, that if he wanted to remain married, he had to just accept her, as she was and so he did. When they arrived home, he became withdrawn and Victoria became more demanding and ruled the home.

Ralph stayed at work longer hours and his business, became more and more successful, but he was depressed and very unhappy about his home life.

Victoria became the social queen of Atlanta, giving lavish dinner parties and was a member of several clubs. She was the center, of her own universe and anyone that knew her had to except that fact or stay out of the way.

Ralph became so beaten down until, the only place he could make decisions was on the job, at the Chamberlain Computer Company..........

EIGHT YEARS LATER
CHAPTER 2

~⁄~

They had a wonderful life together, as long as Ralph said, "yes" to Victoria's every whim. However after eight years of marriage, Victoria had become on top of the socialite ladder in Georgia. Just as Ralph's business, was number one in the computer business and Victoria at her best, something "HAPPEN?"

One day as Victoria came walking in the front door, she was crying hysterically, throwing her purse on the table by the door, making a loud bang. Ralph was sitting in the den, but when he heard Victoria crying and making all the noise, he quickly came into the room. She shouted, "This is going to ruin my social life!" while shaking her finger in Ralph's' face.

Ralph looking puzzled, asks, "What do you mean please, tell me what has happed to cause all this hysteria" She shouted, "I am going to have a baby that is what's wrong." Ralph could not help himself, as he smiled from all the joy of the thought, of having a child, he said, "I will do what ever needs to be done, to help you," as he took her by the arm trying to help her sit down.

Her face was telling him she was absolutely not ready for a baby. Ralph's heart was beating wildly as he said, "Please Victoria tell me, that you are not thinking of getting rid of this baby." "Of course, I am not going to lose my shape or my place in society" she shouted as she crossed her arms and swiftly turning her head away from him.

Ralph nervously said "Victoria this will make you all the more popular now let's call your father with the great news" because he knew the only one she would listen to was her father. Victoria replied, "Do what you like, but my father will only want to make me happy." Ralph shouted, "You are going to have this baby regardless of what you or your father thinks." Victoria stormed out of the room.

Ralph called Mr. Scott to tell him the good news; When Mr. Scott answered the phone, Ralph shouted, "Edward you going to be a grandfather" but instead of saying, "I am proud or I am so happy" to Ralph's surprise he said, "Ralph how is Victoria taking it?" Ralph sadly gave the phone to Victoria and she started crying "Oh father what am I going to do, this is simply dreadful."

Her father said, "Think about it, you will have another reason to have parties and now a baby shower." He continued, "Victoria you two have not been out here in awhile, come out here call your friends about the good news and go shopping." Victoria said, "Father that is a great idea." When she hung up the phone, she said, "Darling we are going to Houston, call the airport we need to leave tonight" as she was going up stairs to pack.

Ralph followed her asking, "Does this mean what I think it means we are keeping the baby?" Victoria ran back and whispered in his ear, "Yes darling, I have to go shopping for the new nursery." Ralph hugged, her as he said, "Thank-You my love, I love you so much." Ralph called his office to tell everyone the good news and had his secretary, to make the arrangements for their flight out.

They flew to Houston that night. The next morning Victoria called her dearest friends, Elizabeth and Ann excited, they came over quickly to go shopping with her. Victoria said, "Now girls you two need to help me with everything, because you have already had children." Elizabeth said, "Of course darling, what are friends for?"

Ann replied, "Victoria I am so glad that you are finally going to have a baby, now I can feel free to talk about my two little girls." Victoria said, "My dear, I did not realize that I made you feel that way." Ann said,"

You didn't, we just did not want you to feel bad, if we brought up our children and you did not have one."

Victoria shouted, "Well honey, that is about to change now, what is first?" Elizabeth said, "Choosing a decorator for the nursery and I know just the one, his name is Paul Thomas." When they arrived at the office of Mr. Thomas, his secretary made an appointment for them. However, the secretary said, "If you would like, you can look through the books, in the conference room before you go."

They went into the conference room and began looking at the books for awhile. Finally, Victoria said, "I have the one, I want for the nursery it is the one with the horses." Elizabeth and Ann agreed that is the best one also. Victoria said, "I would like the nursery to be filled, with the Texas flower and horses."

Later that morning, Mr. Thomas met with the girls and agreed to fly out to do her nursery in a month. Victoria said, "Now that the decisions for the nursery are taken care of, what should we do next." Ann said, "Let's do lunch" Elizabeth said, "Then let's go shopping, at the Mommy's Bouquet, for a wardrobe for you, during your pregnancy."

Victoria said, "Splendid." The girls went out the rest of the day shopping and having a marvelous time. Victoria called, her father on the phone saying, "Father we have accomplished so much today thanks to you, we planned the nursery and shopped for clothes see you tonight." It was about eight o'clock when they arrived home.

Mr. Scott had a party for the occasion and everyone was glad to see Ralph and Victoria again. Victoria wore a black evening gown, that was tea length with matching hat and Ralph wore a black suit with a mint green shirt. Victoria was beautiful before, but now she was radiant, as well. Ralph was absolutely beaming, he was so happy.

However, after about two weeks in Houston, they decided it was time to go back home to Georgia. Mr. Scott said, "Victoria, honey you call me anytime you need me and I will be on the first flight out to Georgia."

Elizabeth and Ann said, "Victoria we will be there on the fifteenth, because we want to see what Mr. Paul Thomas, is going to do to your nursery." However, when Ralph and Victoria came back to Georgia, the pregnancy was being to take its toll, on Victoria. She was sick every morning, having aches and pains she had never had before and now her mood swings were worse than before, if that is possible.

She, shouted at Ralph, "I never knew having a baby could be so bad, I just want to end this pregnancy." Ralph said, "No, the doctor said it will get easier, just give it more time." Finally Elizabeth and Ann arrived, to help her with everything; however Victoria temper, storming around the house and hard words took its toll on them, so they left.

But Ralph was there to take all the hard words and her throwing things at him, but he knew in the end there would be a baby, so he endured it all.

The only thing that Victoria was pleased about, was how the nursery turned out, it was beautiful. When Victoria's father (Mr. Scott) came back for his visit, he hired a new maid, because Victoria had fired the one she had, while in one of her temper tampers, then he hired a cook and a butler also.

Ralph said to him, "Thank-you, for all that you are doing to help Victoria through this time." Mr. Scott replied, "She is my daughter and I will do anything for her." Finally the day came for Victoria to deliver their child. Ralph called his father-in-law and Mr. Scott shouted, "I am on my way." When Mr. Scott arrived at the hospital she was in the delivery room.

Not thinking clearly, from being so protective of his only child, Mr. Scott shouted, at the doctor coming down the hall, "My daughter better not have pain while she is having my grandchild." The doctor smiled, "You must be Victoria's father" as he was thinking, so this is where she gets her temper.

But, Victoria was going through a test of life, which could not be bought away. Mr. Scott would have given anything, to keep his only daughter from going through this. However, no one could have predicted the event that happens next..... Victoria was in the delivery room for a long time.

Ralph and Mr. Scott were waiting for the news of how Victoria and the baby were doing, when the doctor came toward them, with a strange look on his face. They turned looking puzzled, at each other and then back at the doctor.

As The doctor said, "Please sit down, Mr. Chamberlain; I am afraid I have some bad news." Mr. Scott grabbed his chest; Ralph's heart was beating so hard he could hardly breathe, as he shouted, "Please don't tell me, that something has happen to my wife." Mr. Scott, shouted, "Oh no not my child, Victoria."

The doctor quickly assured them saying, "No, it is not your wife, but your son." Ralph had a sigh of relief that Victoria was alright, but franticly looked at the doctor saying, "I have a son?" But, they were puzzled, when the nurse came out smiling, while holding a baby wrapped in a blue blanket saying "Here is your baby Mr. Chamberlain."

Mr. Scott and Ralph looked at the baby, turned to the doctor as Ralph said, "What is wrong with him, he looks perfectly healthy." However, the doctor said, "Not this one, but your other son, your wife had twins." Ralph and Mr. Scott had to sit back down, as they were shocked, with the news, twins.

Mr. Scott shouted, "Doctor how is my daughter taking all of this shocking news? Is the other baby going to live?" The doctor said, "We had to sedate Mrs. Chamberlain to calm her down, you will need to wait awhile before seeing her, she just needs to sleep because of her frail state of mind."

Ralph asks, "May I see my other son now" "Yes but it's bad, let me prepare you, the baby has no upper lip, it is called a cleft palette, I recommend that he be taken to Europe, to the most renown surgeon in the world." Ralph said, "Of course what ever it takes to help my son." Mr. Scott said, "Wait, we have to consider Victoria's decision in this also."

The doctor and Ralph looked at Mr. Scott in disbelief of what he had just said, but they still did not know Victoria like he did. They followed the doctor down the hall to see the baby. Ralph, felt so heavy that he could hardly walk from the grief over his son. The hall seemed to be longer than before, as his mind was spinning around and around.

When the doctor stopped at the door, Ralph walked into the room looked at his baby and gasped for breath, as he began to cry. Mr. Scott refused to go in: instead, he turned and walked back down the hall, to see Victoria. When he walked into the room she was not sleeping, but trying to wake up, thinking she must have had a nightmare.

As She began to wake up, she looked at him and cried, "Father, please help me, I just, can not let anyone know that I had a baby with a deformity." She continued, "Please take him somewhere, anywhere so I will not have to see him." Her father took her by the hand to assure and comfort her.

Ralph walked in just in time to hear her last statement (Please take him somewhere, anywhere so I will not have to see him). Shocked and angry, He said, "What do you mean, we can not abandon our son." Ralph continued, "Victoria, I will do anything you ask, however I will not abandon our son."

Ralph left the hospital to give Victoria time to think about what she was saying, thinking to himself she can not mean what she was saying, but how could she even say such a thing about her own child. Ralph felt overwhelmed by everything, they went to the hospital to have one baby, but now have two, one deformed and Victoria wanted him abandoned, how could all this be taken in, in just a short time?

He felt that they both needed time to take it all in and thinking, "Victoria will understand the need for our baby to get the surgery, he needs." However, the next morning, Ralph returned to the hospital to reason with Victoria, but nothing could change her mind. Mr. Scott said to Ralph, "Victoria is going to have what ever she wants, because she has never known the word "No" and she is not going to start now."

Ralph shouted, "But this is my child's life we are talking about." Victoria had a newspaper on the bed beside her and gave it to Ralph with the birth announcements circled that read: Congratulations to Mr. and Mrs. Ralph Chamberlain on having a baby boy, by the name of Ralph Chamberlain II.

Ralph was angry, as he shouted, "How could you have done this, our other son needs us too." Victoria, said, "I only had one son, I simply refuse to let anyone know that I had a child that is deformed." Teary eyed, Ralph looked at her and ask, "How could you be so cold hearted?" Victoria shouted, "As long as I live, I never want it revealed that I had that other child."

Ralph was filled with rage, as he said, "What do you suppose we do with him, throw him in the trash? He is our son." Victoria demanded, "You can keep the other child, you can also name him, if you would like, but he is to be hidden away so that he can never be seen again." Ralph knew that she had a control over him and he was going to do this thing that was outrageous.

However he changed that day and he knew their life together, would never be the same, as he became withdrawn, to never return for his depression took over his life. Victoria said, "Now go home and make provisions for that child, on the third story of our home to place the deformed child, so no one will know about him, because I will not come home until it is done."

Leaving his feelings bottled up inside, Ralph left the hospital and hired contractors to redo the third story of their home for his other son, who he named Rolf. Ralph instructed the contractors to place sheet rock over all the windows, remove the mirrors, place a fake wall leading from the stairs with a hidden secret door and sound proof walls.

The remodeling took four months. Victoria had gone home to visit her father, while she waited for her home to be completed, because she did not want to ever see her other son. Ralph, called Victoria daily, asking how she and little Ralph, were doing and each day she would say "we are fine if you want us home, finish the house" never asking about her other son.

Ralph found a nurse that would and could care for Rolf her name was Alice Norman; she was one of the nurses that had helped with him at the hospital nursery. Finally the third story was completed, having five bedrooms one which was the nursery of course, but nothing lacking, because Rolf would have the best money could buy, three baths, a full kitchen, dining room and living room.

So there would be no reason for Alice to come down stairs, except to leave knowing that Rolf could never in his life time come down, from the third story of their home. Alice told Ralph, "You know this child could have surgery and be normal as you and I and I think what you two are doing is cruel, to leave him deformed."

Ralph was filled with guilt as he shouted at Alice, "If you want this job, take it as it is or you could leave and not come back." She turned her head looking away from him, because he was filled with anger and she, said, "I will take it, because I have never made this kind of money and I won't say anymore, but you know what I mean."

He looked firmly at her as he, said, "Then I suggest you take care of my baby." Alice moved in that very day. Ralph cried, as he brought Rolf home from the hospital, carrying him gently up the stairs knowing it was his only trip upstairs, never to return into the real world again. Nonetheless, He wanted equal care for the boys, but knew Rolf was the same as an orphan.

But now, it was time for the rest of the family to return home and Ralph had to go downstairs to welcome them home. The next day, Mr. Scott arrived home with Victoria and Ralph II. Ralph was excited to see them; he went out to the car and carried baby Ralph inside. When Victoria walked inside Ralph looked at her and said, "Pet I have named our other son, Rolf what do you think of that name?"

Victoria stared, at him for a while and said, "Well darling, I have already named our son Ralph II the only son I have, if you have another one, name him what you like." Ralph's heart was heavy with sadness, that his wife could be so cold toward her own son. He said, "Victoria, I will promise you as long as I live, I will never say that Rolf is your son again, but he is mine."

Victoria placed her hands on her hips, with her eye brows raised and shouted, "Don't ever say anything, about your other child to me again and as long as I live, I will never see him or admit that he even exist."

Mr. Scott shouted, "This is suppose to be a happy time, now let's get Ralph II settled in his new room. Now where is it?"

Victoria said, "Father follow me, you will love our new baby's room." Ralph watched them take Ralph II to his new room, like there was nothing wrong with what they were doing to Rolf, but now the pretense would begin.

Victoria looked back at Ralph, and asks, "Is the other one put away so I can't see it." Ralph, looked at her with discuss and replied, "Yes Rolf is in his nursery and you will not have to worry about anyone seeing him EVER!"

Victoria shrugged her shoulders and said, "Good" as she continued, walking to Ralph II's room to get him settled. However, Ralph went up to the third story, to check on Alice and Rolf. When he entered into the hallway, he could hear Rolf crying, he quickly went into the nursery to check on him and he was alone, he picked him up, to comfort him and looked for Alice.

He found her sitting in the den reading a book, he asks, "What do you think you are doing? Couldn't you hear Rolf crying?" Alice shrugged her shoulder, as she smugly replied, "Yes, but it is not going to hurt him to cry." Ralph said roughly," You let me know right now, if you still want this job, because I will find someone else today, if you don't want to be here."

Alice became teary eyed, "Yes I would like to keep this job." Ralph said, "Then I suggest you take care of my baby" as he placed Rolf into her arms and went back down stairs. Alice knew she could not find another job that paid as well, so she cared for Rolf. After that day Ralph went up to Rolf's room daily to check on him, but he never picked him up again, he felt there was no need, because he could never fully be anyone's son.

Mr. Scott stayed for a week, never entering the upstairs to see Rolf, his own grandson, or even asking about him. Before he left however, he asks Ralph "I am asking you to never mention Rolf, to Victoria again" Ralph answered, "Alright" and that was the last words spoken between them, before Mr. Scott left for home.

Now, it had been two weeks since the babies came home and Ralph was making his daily visit upstairs to see Rolf. However, as he quietly entered Rolf's room, so he would not wake him, if he was sleeping, he saw Alice holding a pillow, over the crib and slowly toward Rolf's head. Ralph was in shock for a moment, before it sunk in, that she was trying to kill his baby.

Ralph screamed, "Stop, Stop!" Shocked, Alice dropped the pillow on the floor and tried to run out of the room. He took her by the hand and pulled her into the den, where he was going to call the police; however she got away from him, ran into the hallway, then opened the fake sound proof door, that leads to the down stairs.

Enraged, Ralph grabbed her by the hair and pulled her back into the den again. Alice was screaming "Help, Help me please somebody, Help me!" as she was filled with fear for her life. Victoria heard her screams and ran upstairs. As she came into the hallway, she saw Ralph pulling Alice by her hair, into the den and she looked at Alice's face, as it was filled with fear.

Shocked and surprised at what she was seeing, she shouted, "Ralph what you are doing?" Ralph held on to Alice's arm, turned to Victoria and shouted, "I am calling the police, because Alice just tried to kill our son." Victoria shouted, "No Ralph, you can not call the police, because they will find out about me having a deformed child."

Angry, Ralph shouted back at her, "Victoria is that all you can think about is yourself, this woman just tried to kill our son." She shouted, LET HER GO!" Therefore, Ralph let Alice go, then Victoria said to her, "Alice you have to promise to leave town, never return or speak of this child and if you return, we will call the police, do you understand."

Alice replied, "I agree, but I am telling you now, there is no one that is going to want to care for that child." Ralph still enraged, shouted, "Get out quickly, before I change my mind." Alice quickly ran out of the house. Ralph looked at Victoria still filled with anger, shouted, "Your heart is made of ice."

She replied, "Do you honestly think I care, what you think" and she turned away and went back down stairs. Ralph stayed upstairs to care for Rolf, feeling overwhelmed in his decision, to keep this baby. Not only was he alone in this, but now he had to go find a nurse to care for Rolf. He called the hospital and spoke with the doctor that delivered the twins, but did not tell the doctor, that he had not had the surgery.

The doctor said, "I recommend a nurse, by the name of Ruby Howard, she was married to a friend of mine, who is also a doctor." The doctor continued, "Their marriage ended in divorce after the lost of their only child; a son who lived only six months and died of SIDS. The grief was too much for them and it broke up their marriage."

When Ralph met with Ruby, his face was filled with sadness and it showed. Ruby asks, "Why are you so sad?" He began to explain the situation, "Well I need you to care for one of my twins, a son named Rolf, my wife is raising the other son downstairs, and you will be living upstairs in an apartment fully furnished. If you need anything just ask."

Ralph said, "My wife will only accept one of our sons but not the other" Ruby was puzzled, and asks, "Why won't your wife accept her own child?" However, Ralph did not explain that Rolf was deformed; only that Victoria would only accept one of their children. Ruby saw that she was not going to get an answer from him, so she decided to take the job on blind faith.

She said, "Mr. Chamberlain, this may be a good thing for me to come into new surroundings, so I can begin to heal from my own loss of my child." Ralph said, "I agree, our twins are only four and a half months old, so it will be easy to care for Rolf." When Ruby arrived, Victoria was waiting with her hand on her hip, just inside the living room saying "Well I have been waiting."

Ralph whispered to Ruby "My wife is not as easy to get along with as me and for that I am sorry." Victoria said to Ruby, "I am so glad you are here, because I sure did not want to go upstairs to check on that other baby." Ruby was shocked, at the hardness of a mother's heart toward her baby. Victoria said, "Ruby would you like to see my baby, or would you like to go straight upstairs to care for Mr. Chamberlain's baby."

Startled, Ruby said, "I do not understand why you are making a difference in these babies." Victoria said, "Oh I see Mr. Chamberlain has not told you everything, however here is our baby, Ralph II." She picked him up and placed him into Ruby's arms and Ruby said, "Oh he is simply beautiful" then she gave the baby back to, Victoria.

Ruby turned to look at Ralph and said, "I think we need to go upstairs to check on Rolf." Ralph said, "Follow me" as he began to walk upstairs, Ruby was behind him. But when they got to the top of the stairs Ruby, watched Ralph push in this door that looked like part of the wall; looking puzzled, she asks, "Why is the door made to look like the wall?"

Ralph replied, "Because, we do not want anyone to know about the third story of our home." Then they walked into a small hallway, to a door that was locked, Ralph gave Ruby a key, she unlocked it and then they went to Rolf's room. Ruby walked over to the crib however, when she saw Rolf she was shocked, she turned and ran out into the hallway.

Ralph went after her saying, "Please come back" Ruby was anger, as she said, "Mr. Chamberlain, did you honestly think I would not take the job, if you told me that your child had a cleft palette." She continued, "I am a nurse and I know how to care for Rolf, but why haven't you two taken him in for surgery? He can be as anyone else with the surgery."

Ralph said, "It is not that simple, my wife has told everyone that we only had one child and she will never agree for Rolf, to have the surgery, now will you take the job or not." She went back into the nursery, picked Rolf up because he was crying and rocked him to sleep. Ralph said, "I will leave you two alone" as he walked back down stairs.

She looked at him while he slept and knew she was needed, feeling so much compassion for him, she instantly fell in love with him, as if he was her own son. Time began to pass by and in Ruby's heart; she became Rolf's mother, just as Rolf bonded with her. She tried to tell Ralph and Victoria that the doctors could fix Rolf's face, but to no avail.

Victoria had said, "I have already told everyone that we only had one child and that is final" Ruby shouted, "You, are the coldest person I have ever met." She never bothered them again, about Rolf's problem. But Ruby felt alone and frustrated, but refused to give up hope that maybe, someday she could get help for him.

Ruby rocked, loved and spoiled Rolf and Ralph stopped coming to see him after awhile, because he saw that he was well taken care for, Rolf was only eight months old. One day while downstairs, Ruby asks, "Ralph why there are no mirrors in the upstairs" Ralph replied, "Because we never want Rolf to know what he looks like."

She replied, "But don't you realize that if he sees himself later, he will be devastated and filled with confusion." Filled with guilt and anger, Ralph shouted, "Well you have to make sure that never happens, don't you." Ruby became teary eyed and knew she was not able to continue the conversation, because she would began to cry and not stop, so she went back upstairs to care for Rolf.

Rolf began to grow and began to walk at only ten months old, later when he was about two years old, Ruby began teaching him to communicate with his hands, and because of his deformity he could not talk. Ruby did everything she could to help Rolf live a healthy, happy life learning all the things a child his age is suppose to know.

It was hard to teach some things, because she needed him, to see himself in the mirror and understand how to speak, by watching himself in the mirror, but that was not to be. Rolf did not know what he looked like, because he had never seen himself, because all of the mirrors were removed before he was born.

His world existed of the third story of the Chamberlain home and he knew nothing of the outside. Nevertheless, he was a happy child and Ruby taught him well, as well as she could up to age five could be taught, but then something happened.........

FIVE YEARS LATER
CHAPTER 3

⟡

The Chamberlain family had been peaceful now, for five years as Ruby had become part of the family. She would come down stairs, to spent short visits with Ralph II, as he would always greet her with a hug. Ralph and Victoria loved her as a member of the family however; the home still was separated with words never spoken of Rolf.

Ruby had become Rolf's mother, the only one he had ever known. She had taught him sign language because of his deformity, he could not speak and he called her, "Mother" with his hands. She had been a part of both boys life, with potty training, teaching them to ride a tricycle, playing games and reading stories to them, separately of course.

However, one day as Ruby was going up stairs, she did not realize that little Ralph, was following her. Now he had been told many times, "Do not go upstairs with Ms. Ruby," but today he was going anyway. He watched her open the fake door, then he went back down stairs and waited for her to come back down, when she did he ran back up stairs, opened the fake door and entered the third story.

Ralph II walked down the hall into the kitchen, where he found some cookies and milk as five year olds' will do. He said, "Oh boy this is fun," then he ran down the hall, to another room. However, when he saw something or someone, he was not sure, because he had never seen anyone with a deformity before. He was afraid and confused, by what he saw; it was Rolf jumping on the bed.

Rolf stopped, as he was looking at Ralph II with fear and confusion too, because he did not remember seeing any other person other than, Ruby. He did not even know that there were other people in the world. They screamed for a second, and then they both realized, with an instant understanding, that they did not have to be afraid of each other.

Ralph II climbed on the bed with Rolf and they both jumped on it, together. They had instantly become friends however, after they stopped jumping; Ralph II asks "What happened to you, why do you look like that?" as he pointed to Rolf's face. Of course Rolf was confused, because he did not understand that question, he did not know he was deformed, and had never seen himself.

Rolf was thinking, mommy (Ruby) never said, anything like that.

Nevertheless, they were playing and both enjoying the attention; they both were getting from their new playmate. Thirty minutes later the twins had become best friends. However, Ruby came walking into the room and was shocked, seeing both boys jumping on the bed and eating cookies together and enjoying play.

Ruby became very nervous and upset knowing that the Chamberlain's were going to blame her for this. She took Ralph, by the arm and gently lead him into the hall and said, "Ralph your mommy and daddy are going to be very upset with you for being up here in Rolf's room." He looked up at her with tears as his lips trembled, he said, "But Ms. Ruby he is my best friend now, and I don't have anyone else to play with, please let me stay."

She reluctantly, replied, "Alright, but only a little while longer, because your mommy and daddy will be upset, about you being up here." Ralph II looked at her again, with his little sad eyes and asks, "Why?" She took him back into Rolf's room and explained to both of them, "Well you see this is your brother and I think you two should be able to play together."

She continued, "However if your mommy and daddy find out that you were up here, they will make me go away and you will never be able to see Rolf again." Ralph II asks again, "Why?" Before Ruby thought about it, she muttered the words, "I wish your mommy and daddy would have the surgery, Rolf needs for his face."

Ralph asks, "What do you mean Ms. Ruby?" and Rolf looking at her with confusion; She gasped as she realized she had said, too much, "I am sorry I said that, little boys do not need to know what grown ups talk about." Ralph II said, "I will help him, tell me how" She smiled at him and said, "Ok when you grow up, you can become a doctor and fix your brother's face."

By this time, Rolf was getting upset and confused and started to cry, Ruby picked him up and sat him in her lap saying, "Everything is alright" wrapping her arms around him. Ralph II was looking up at her as he said; "Ok" Ruby asks, "What do you mean?" "Ok" he replied, "Ok I will be a doctor, when I grow up and fix Rolf."

Ruby did not realize that she had just set the wheels in motion for his life, that very moment. Ralph and Victoria were downstairs looking frantically for Ralph II, after awhile they looked at each other thinking the same thing "he is upstairs." So they slowly walked up the stairs, all the while hoping this was not the case.

However, when they got upstairs and into the hallway, Victoria held her stomach saying, "You go in I simply can not, I think I am going to be sick," but then, they heard the voices of both Ruby and Ralph II. Victoria sighed with relief that Ralph II was alright, but angry at the same time, because he was upstairs she shouted, "Ralph II dear, come to mommy."

Ruby became filled with fear and panic, because she just knew she was about to be fired and separated from Rolf. So Ruby quickly, took Ralph II, by the hand and they walked out into the hallway, together. Ruby looked back at Rolf and signed stay in the room. When Victoria had Ralph II close enough to her, she grabbed him by the arm and started taking him downstairs while shouting, "Ruby you are fired I can not believe that you let this happen."

Ralph stayed upstairs, looking at Ruby asking, "Ruby how could this have happened?" She was crying, "Please don't fire me, I did not know Ralph II was up here, until I came back and found them playing together." Ralph snapped at her, "Playing together" Ruby sniveled, as she said, "Yes they did not understand, why they could not play, after all they are just children" as she wiped the tears from her eyes.

Ralph took a deep breath, as he said, "You are not fired, we will work this out somehow, but the boys have to stay separated." They looked behind them, Rolf had tears coming down his cheeks and looking up at them with confusion written on his face, as he was wondering, "what was going on." He signed, "Who is this person and who was that other person and where is Ralph II?" as he pointed at his father.

Ralph watched, as Rolf was signing and asks, "What is he doing?" She said, "He is signing, because he can't talk with his deformity" Ralph asks, and "What did he say?" She said, "He asks who you where and who Victoria was and where is Ralph II?" He smiled and said, "Ruby you have done a remarkable job with him, thank you."

Ralph continued, "But I have to go downstairs now, to do some damage control" he turned and went back downstairs, to speak to Victoria and Ralph II. Ruby stayed upstairs with Rolf, to comfort him and try to explain that he could not see Ralph II again and still not let him know, that he was different, but it was hard to explain something, she did not understand herself.

However when Ralph got back downstairs, Ralph II was jumping up and down crying "Why can't I play with my best friend, he knows how to have fun." Victoria looked at Ralph coming down stairs, she shouted, "I want Ruby out of this house today" "No she is staying, she did not take Ralph II upstairs, she found him there and she is not fired."

Victoria looked at Ralph II asking him, "How did you get upstairs?" He said, "Mommy that is easy, I watched Ms. Ruby when she wasn't looking and I did the same after she came back down stairs, please let me go back upstairs to play." Victoria shouted "No you can ever go back upstairs again!" as she picked him up and sat him on the couch beside her.

Ralph II cried and cried, as he fell across his mother's lap, "please let me play with my brother, he is my best friend, please let me go back." Ralph stepped in saying, "Victoria he already knows about him, what can it hurt for them to play together now." After awhile, she stood him up in front of her as she said, "Alright, but if you ever tell anyone about Rolf, I will send him and Ms. Ruby away do you understand, what I am saying?"

Ralph II chuckled from happiness as he said, "Yes mommy I promise I will never tell anyone, so can I go back upstairs to play now?" Ralph said, "Ralph II it is time for bed now, so you can play again tomorrow say good night now." Ralph II was filled with excitement and said, "Oh I can't wait until tomorrow, so I will go to sleep fast ok" while he was running to his room.

After Ralph II had left the room, Victoria looked at Ralph with contempt as she said, "I hate you, for bringing that other child into this house, and he has brought nothing, but grief, why did you do that?" Ralph's anger came out in his voice, as he said, "How could you be so cruel, as to let this other child live with a deformity, that could be corrected so easily and he could live a normal life, with the rest of his family."

Victoria's said sarcastically, "You are not going to blame me for all of it, you allowed him to do the same, why?" He stormed out of the room shouting, "You are right, this has to stop, and I am going to correct this right now, by calling the doctor and having my child's surgery, so he can live in the real world with the rest of us."

Victoria ran after him, "Please don't do this I will stop, if you will just not call the doctor, I know it is my fault entirely, but please just leave him as he is." Ralph put the phone down saying; "I will not call tonight, but we have to talk more about this later" she walked away muttering, "We will see."

However, the next morning Ruby came into Rolf's room as she had every morning, but this morning was different.... She sat down in the rocking chair and Rolf sits in her lap and began playing with the locket, she had around her neck. But, Ruby had forgotten that the locket had a mirror inside of it.

Rolf opens the locket seeing a picture of Ralph II, on one side, then he saw his reflection and suddenly he realizes that it is himself and knew he was different. Just as he began to scream, Ralph II opens the sound proof door and Rolf's screams could be heard down stairs. Rolf was filled with fear and confusion. Ruby was trying to calm him saying, "It is ok, please Rolf its ok" but to no avail and she could not get the mirror from his hand.

Ralph and Victoria heard Rolf's screams and came running upstairs, to find out what had happen. But before they could get up there, Ralph II ran in his room asking, "What is wrong with him, why is he screaming?" Before she could answer, Ralph and Victoria came rushing into the room, somewhat breathless shouting, "What is going on?" Ruby said, "He just realized that he is different from you or me."

Victoria saw Rolf for the first time and when he looked up at her, she quickly ran out of the room, her heart racing. Still sitting in the rocking chair, Ruby looked at Ralph, as she held up the locket with the mirror in it. Ralph snatched it from her; all the while his heart was aching for Rolf, as he was still screaming.

Nevertheless, Ralph took Rolf out of her lap and placed him on the floor.

He then pulled Ruby, by the arm out of the room, into the hall. Ralph II was crying with Rolf sitting, on the floor in the room together, neither understanding what was going on. Ralph held the locket in front of Ruby's face as he shouted, "Why did you let Rolf see this locket?"

She was crying, "I would never do anything to purposely hurt Rolf, as you well know." Victoria took her by the arm and turned her around toward her, shouting, "It does not matter if it was done on purpose or not you are fired." Ralph held up his hand toward Victoria, as he shouted, "Wait we can't leave Rolf alone he needs Ruby, she has become his mother."

Victoria shouted, "I want her out of this house today!" Ralph II came running out of Rolf's room screaming, "No, No we love Ruby, she can't leave please mommy, don't make her leave" as tears flowed down his face. Victoria took Ralph II by the arm and pulled him down stairs. Rolf ran out of his room and wrapped his arms around Ruby's waist, crying hysterically.

Ralph's heart ached for him, however Ralph told her, "Ruby I don't see how I can let you stay, when Victoria is so set on you going." Ruby looked at him, her eyes filled with tears begging, "How can you make me go, when Rolf needs me so, I am the only mother, this child has ever known or ever will know, Please let me stay."

Ralph walked away from her without another word and walked down stairs, where Victoria was waiting for him. She said, "Where is Ruby; packing?" Ralph said, "No we need to talk" "No there is nothing to talk about, I told you I wanted Ruby out today and I mean just that." Ralph shouted, "Why can't we call the doctor and have Rolf fixed, so he can live a normal life, what is wrong with you, you don't have to be his mother, Ruby could stay and raise him as her own."

Ralph II shouted, "Yes mommy let Ruby stay and let the doctor fix Rolf, so he can look better" as he wrapped his arms around her waist. Victoria shouted, "Now see what you have done; now our son feels he has to take sides, I want her out!" Ralph II said, "When I get big I will be a doctor and fix him."

Victoria stared at Ralph, as she shouted, "Decide now Ruby or me!" Ralph knew she was serious and he had to make Ruby go, or Victoria would leave and take Ralph II with her. He slowly went back upstairs to tell Ruby, his heart was heavy and he knew what he was about to do was very wrong but his love for Victoria out weighed anything or anyone else including his own son.

Victoria took Ralph II away from the house, so he would not be traumatized anymore than he already was, by seeing Ruby leaving. When Ralph walked back inside Rolf's room, Ruby was rocking him to sleep, his arms around her neck, and soft music playing. Rolf had calmed down and Ruby had assured him that everything was going to be alright. But, when she looked up at Ralph's face she realized, everything was not alright.

He sadly said, "I am sorry but you will have to leave, because my wife said it is you or her and I am not going to lose my wife." Ruby put her finger on her lips, to ask Ralph to hush for a moment, as she slowly got up and began laying Rolf on the bed, as not to upset him again. She softly said, "Let's talk in the hallway."

So they stepped into the hallway and she asks Ralph, "What about Rolf what is going to happen to him." Ralph said, "You don't have to worry about him, I will hire him another nurse." Ruby looked at him with confusion saying, "How could you bring me here, let me fall in love with your abandoned child and allow him to love me, as his mother and then tear out our hearts, by separating us over one stupid mistake, on my part."

She continued, "Isn't anyone in your family allowed, to make a mistake and be forgiven please don't punish your own child, for my mistake; if you make me leave, Rolf will never get over it." Ralph said firmly, "Pack your bags, you have to leave today." She knew she couldn't win and knew she was going to have to leave, so she began to pack, with tears flowing down her cheeks.

When she was finished, Ralph was waiting in the hall to make sure she was leaving. However Rolf saw her with her bags, ran and held on to her, she hugged him saying, "Rolf I have to leave, but you are going to be alright" while tears where flowing down both of their faces. He began signing, "Please, please don't leave, I love you and I will be a good boy."

Ralph took her bags and threw them down stairs, then he took Rolf back into his room and said, "Stay here." He then took Ruby by the arm and began taking her downstairs, but Rolf came running after her, screaming and crying. Ralph took him back and closed the door and locked it, behind him.

Rolf was beating on the door, begging Ruby to come back, but the sound proof door was closed and his cries unheard. Ruby left the

Chamberlain home with her heart-broken. Ralph called and hired another nurse, by the name of Gloria, to care for Rolf. She came to the Chamberlain home and Victoria and Ralph were satisfied, seeing she was a good person.

Two days later, Ralph was sitting at the table drinking his coffee, reading the newspaper and he gashed, as he stated, "I can't breathe" he got up from the table walking around holding his chest, trying to breathe. Victoria shouted, "What is it," she took the paper and read the front page. Ruby had committed suicide by taking an over dose of sleeping pills.

She left a note reading: I lost my child and I can't go on my heart is too heavy for me to bear. Filled with guilt and shame, Ralph shouted, "This is our fault, Ruby was a good person and she loved our son!" Victoria yelled back, "Well she is gone now, don't dwell on it." Ralph snapped sarcastically, "Why am I shocked, I knew you where cold hearted, but this doesn't bother you?" standing, as he looked at her for an answer.

She said, "Why should it, I didn't give her the sleeping pills?" as she was looking ever so serious at him. As he was filled with anger, guilt and shame Ralph walked upstairs, to check on Rolf and the new nurse. However, when he walked into Rolf's room, he was sitting alone, Ralph asks, "Where is Ms. Gloria?"

Rolf signed, "I don't care" Ralph walked into the den, where she was sitting in a chair, reading a book. He asks, "How is everything going with Rolf." She looked at him saying, "That is one sad little boy." She continued, "It is going to take a long time for him, to let anyone close to him, all he asks for is his "mommy Ruby."

Ralph said, "Ruby was the nurse before you." She said sharply, "Not to him, she was his mother!" as she continued to read her book. He said, "Yes I know" holding his head down, from the guilt and turned away walking back downstairs. Filled with so much emotion, Ralph left that day and never went back upstairs again.

After awhile Victoria and Ralph agreed, for Ralph II to go back upstairs, to play with Rolf, because he never let up, on his begging, giving them grief to see Rolf again. Ralph II began to go up everyday; they knew he was alright, because Gloria was good to him too. However, Gloria was nothing like Ruby, she did not want to be friends with Ralph and Victoria; in fact she did not even like them at all, so she stayed to herself taking care of Rolf alone except for the visits from Ralph II.

Nevertheless, Rolf would not let himself get close to her, for fear of her leaving too. The two boys would remember what Ruby had said, "You two brothers should always be best friends and care for each other." Later Ralph II had to go to school. Rolf would ask to go, but Gloria taught him. Ralph II asks, "Mommy, could I please have a camera."

Ralph II took pictures of everything, so Rolf would have some idea of the outside world. He asks, "Could you buy Rolf a TV" so they did, but the nurse had to hid him in the other room, so the cable guy could not see him. But, some how that wasn't enough, so Ralph II brought flowers in for Rolf to see, feel and smell.

Ralph II thought it would help, but it made Rolf realize, that he was missing something and he became angry. So, Ralph II did not bring anymore of the outside world into Rolf's world. Rolf asks if he could go out like Ralph II, but to no avail, so he gave up after awhile. Later, Victoria told Ralph II, "You have to take piano lessons; every well bred boy has to learn to play the piano."

Ralph II said, "Only if you buy Rolf a piano, too" "Who will teach him?" Victoria shouted, with a frown on her face. Ralph II smiled, "I will teach him, I don't mind." So Victoria calls and ordered two grand pianos to be delivered to their home; however, the nurse had to hide Rolf again for the movers to carry one upstairs.

When the lessons began Ralph II would run upstairs afterward and teach Rolf what he learned that day and they practiced, laughing and enjoying life together. Once they learned to play the piano, Victoria said, "Now you have to learn to play the violin." Ralph II said, "Mother only if you buy two violins" "Fine I don't mind buying two, as long as no one can see, you know who" she shouted and walked out of the room.

She ordered the violins and they learned to play. They studied hard and the time was going by and Ralph II said, "Rolf we have to study hard and learn everything we need to know to, become a doctor to fix your face and then, you can walk out of this house with me." He said, "Where will we go?"

Ralph II said, "Anywhere you would like, because I want to show you all the things you have missed" and they hugged. Then the computer age came about, so Ralph II asks, "Mother could you please order two computers, we need them" so she did, without question. Ralph II and Rolf did their research, for the surgery and for the first time Rolf saw others, like him.

Another world opened up to them on the internet, where they learned so much and were more advanced than other kids their age. Later it was time for the prom, at Ralph II School and he had to learn to dance, so he ordered a DVD for Rolf to learn to dance with him, upstairs in Rolf's place of course.

Rolf asks, "Why are we learning to dance?" Ralph II without thinking said, "Because the prom is coming up and we have to dance with the girls, silly." Then he realized, what he had just said, and Rolf pushed him down signing, "You are cruel, like everyone else." Ralph II tired to apologize, but Rolf would not hear it and did not want to speak to him, for two days.

Ralph II said, "I won't go to the prom, if you do not want me to" looking at Rolf for approval. But Rolf signed, "No go, because I want to see pictures, of what it is like to go to the prom. So Ralph II went, but he didn't stay long, because he felt guilty for leaving Rolf. However, he got some good pictures to show him.

Rolf had pictures of everything, from the time they were five years old and Ralph II had taken the first photos. In the beginning of course the photo's were not very good, because Ralph II had taken the pictures upside down, sideways and so forth, but he was trying to show Rolf, the outside world.

The photo's were of butterflies, flowers, grass, a dog, a cat and everything else that Ralph II saw, he would take photo's of for Rolf. So Rolf had photos hanging all over the walls upstairs. From the time they were five until now thirteen years later there were many, many photo's taken, for Rolf to know all about Ralph's experience of the outside world.

However, time was ticking by and it was time for graduation. Rolf graduated from home-school; Ralph got him, a cap and gown like his so he would not feel left out. But, Ralph of course had to walk up the steps, to the stage outside at the ball field. A speech was given for the seniors, and Ralph was given a scholarship for college.

Everyone was shouting for joy and at the end threw their caps, into the air. And of course Ralph brought home a video, of the event. However, he did not tell Rolf about the party afterward, with all his friends. When Rolf saw the video, of Ralph II's graduation and how his mother and father hugged, him and smiling, with pride throughout the tape, his jealously enraged him.

He angrily, signed to Ralph II, "This is not fair, you always get everything and everyone loves you, what about me?" as he started throwing things and signing for him, to leave. Ralph left for a few days, but when he returned Rolf was happy to see him. Ralph said, "Rolf you shouldn't treat me like that, because I am doing everything I can to help you, I am even becoming a plastic surgeon, so I can fix your face and then you, can walk out of here with me."

Rolf hugged, him and signed, "I am sorry, just don't leave me" "Don't worry I will never leave you." Ralph said, "Rolf, listen to me you do understand that it will take a long time for me, to become a plastic surgeon don't you?" Rolf signed, "Yes, but I want to become one too." Ralph said, "Alright we will learn together, I will teach you everything I know, as I learn it."

Ralph continued, "But Rolf I will have to go away for awhile to a college, but I will e-mail you, everyday." Rolf signed, "Don't go" "I have to go, so I can learn from people that do not live around here, alright, please be patient." So the time came for Ralph to leave for college however, that day he was trying to tell Rolf good-bye Rolf went into a rage throwing things, so Ralph had to go without saying, good-bye.

Heartbreaking as it was to leave, Ralph understood Rolf was feeling abandoned all over again, first by their parents and then, by Ruby even though it was not her fault, but now he felt, as though Ralph would leave and not come back. Rolf fell into a deep depression and refused to eat, until he was reassured, of Ralph's return.

However, after a few weeks Ralph returned, to let Rolf know how things were going at college. But, Rolf was so weak he could not even hold his head up. Ralph saw him and began to cry, looking at him he said, "Rolf why are you doing this to yourself?" Rolf signed, "I though you were not coming back."

Ralph brought Rolf some soup and crackers saying, "Rolf you have to eat" so he did. Then he asks, "Rolf why didn't you answer my e-mails?" Rolf looked shocked, because he had not even thought about the e-mails, smiling he signed, "I forgot about them." Ralph put his hand on Rolf's shoulder and said, "It is ok this time, but please reply to them, because we have a lot to learn, ok."

Rolf signed, "It won't happen again, I am alright now, it's ok for you to go back to college, because I want to learn and we both can walk out of here together, as you said." Ralph smiled, "That sounds like a winner to me" and Ralph went back to college and they e-mailed and wrote letters daily.

Finally the day comes that Ralph II has the opportunity to finish his internship, with the most renowned plastic surgeon in the world. So he comes home, to share the good news with his family. He first tells his mother and father, Victoria smiled saying, "That is great news dear, anything to get you away from, you know who."

Ralph said, "Son I am very proud of you go and fulfill your dream" "My dream is what it has always been and that is the fix my brother's face, so he can make his own dream, whatever that maybe. Now if you two will excuse me, I have to go tell him the good news" as he began walking upstairs. Victoria shouted, "You do what you want, as long as no one knows about him."

However, when Ralph II tells Rolf, he asks, "How long will you be gone this time?" Ralph II said, "Rolf I have to go to Paris, France, so that will take two years, but when I return home, I will be ready to do what should have been done shortly after your birth." But, Rolf would not hear anymore, he angrily signed, "Take me out today, take me with you to Paris, I refuse to stay here any longer."

Then Rolf jumped on Ralph II and started choking him, because he felt that Ralph II was telling him good-bye forever. Ralph II fought with him and got away and ran to the sound proof door, as he opened it he was yelling, "Help father, Help." Ralph ran up the stairs and helped Ralph II Nevertheless, Ralph II turned to Rolf and said, "I promise I am coming back for you" and they closed the door behind them.

Ralph, looked at Ralph II saying, "Son forget about him and go make your own life, he will be alright." But Ralph II said, "Dad I will be back and I am going to take him out of here, fix his face and he will have the life, he has always had the right to have. He packed his bags and his father and mother took him to the airport.

Ralph wrapped his arms around him and whispered, "I love both of my boys be safe." Victoria said, "Do well with your life and don't worry about anyone, but yourself and you can make it." Ralph boarded the plane and was on his way to Paris, France.............

RALPH ARRIVES IN PARIS
CHAPTER 4

R alph arrives in Paris, with enthusiasm and excitement, however exhausted from jetlag. When he comes off the plane, he is met by a man named, Mr. Vance (an elderly distinguished gentleman). Mr. Vance introduced himself to Ralph then asks, "Mr. Chamberlain would you like to go straight to your hotel, or to a restaurant, for a bite to eat?"

Ralph replied, "Please take me, to the Hotel De Ville first so I can rest for a while." He looked at the Paris view of the Museede Notre Dame, Institute du Mone Arabe, and Musee Adam Mickiewicz, on the way it was beautiful. Mr. Vance said, "Ralph I will be back to pick you up at seven this evening for dinner" and he left.

However, that evening when Mr. Vance and Ralph walked outside Ralph looked for the car, but did not see one. Mr. Vance began to laugh, "Ha, Ha" "Ralph in Paris we ride bikes for short distances." While he was still speaking a group of bikers rode up and had two exacter bikes, for them.

So, they got on the bikes and rode over a small bridge that had a beautiful waterfall garden, on the other side of it, on the way to the restaurant "Du Pre." Mr. Vance announced, "I will show you a good time in Paris tonight, Ralph." The restaurant had beautiful music, great food and many beautiful ladies, so they danced most of the night and had a wonderful time. Everyone seemed to be happy, in Paris.

Ralph was thinking "Now I know why they call this the most romantic city in the world, romance is everywhere you look." He rested all the next day and ordered room service, as he observed the maids and the rest of the staff singing and enjoying life, as everyone seemed to in Paris. Finally, Friday came and he was excited that he was going to meet, Dr. Edward Kennedy the most renowned surgeon in the world.

When Ralph arrived at the hospital, he was introduced to Dr. Kennedy, (a tall-slender, handsome man, with light brown hair, a touch of gray and hazel eyes) not at all, what Ralph II was expecting him to look like. Dr. Kennedy looked at Ralph and said, "You are much younger than I expected you to be."

Ralph said, "Dr. Kennedy I am twenty-five years old and I am honored to meet you, at last." (Ralph was tall six-foot three, muscular build, with black hair and blue eyes a very handsome young man.) Dr. Kennedy and Ralph became friends, instantly. Dr. Kennedy then introduced Ralph II to all of his staff.

After working together a few weeks, he said to Ralph, "You may call me Edward, because I consider you a very special friend." He replied, "Thank-You, doctor I will and I am glad I have a friend like you." That night Ralph wrote letters and sent photo's home to Rolf, about everything and how, Dr. Kennedy had become one of the most important people in his life however, he let Rolf know, he was the most important one.

After six months of study, hard work and writing letters to Rolf daily, Ralph needed a break, so he took a week off. One day, during that week he decided to go for a bike ride, to tour the city. After riding for a while Ralph, stopped at the restaurant DuPre. He went in and sat at the table in the back corner, so he could be alone and clear his mind for a while.

However, after a couple of minutes he heard a soft voice asking him, "Sir are you ready to order?" When he looked up he, instantly fell in love, with the girl that was speaking to him. She was tall slender, beautifully shaped, with long blonde hair and her eyes were sky-blue. Ralph gazed, at her, as he asks, "What do you recommend" She said softly, "I recommend the special of the day, because I made it" as she giggled.

He replied, "That will be fine" she walked away and after awhile, she was back with the meal, as she placed it on the table in front of him; he said, "My name is Ralph Chamberlain II may I please know your name," as he was sitting back in his chair to hear her answer. She replied, "My name is Rachel Royal."

Ralph asks, "May I ask where you are from, because you do not have a French accent?" Rachel smiled, as she said, "I am from Oklahoma, in the United States and where are you from?" Ralph replied, "I am from Atlanta, Georgia." Rachel turned, as she was walking away she said, "I am sorry, but I have to work now."

Ralph reached out and touched her hand asking, "May I please see you after work sometime." She turned looking at him saying; "I get off in one hour, if you would like to wait" he smiled and said, "I'll wait." So they went for a bike ride and talked. Ralph said, "Please tell me about you" as they were walking their bikes, over the bridge.

Rachel began, "I grew up in Lawton, Oklahoma my father (Daniel Royal) was a train engineer and my mother Ruth was a housewife, until my father was killed in a train wreck, when I was eight years old." He said, "Oh I am sorry about your father" she continued, "My mother then became, a bookkeeper in a restaurant, where I had free rein to play."

"The owner of the restaurant took a special interest, in teaching me how to cook and as I grew up I realized, I wanted to learn more, be a chef someday and own a restaurant, not just work in one." She continued, "That is what brought me to Paris, I am now working with, one of the greatest chef's in the world."

Then she turned and looked at him, as she said; "Now, you know all about me, now, it is your turn tell me about you." They sat down on a bench and Ralph said, "There is not much to tell, I grew up in Atlanta Georgia, my father Ralph Chamberlain, is the owner and founder of the Chamberlain Computer Company and my mother is a member of all the social clubs" and he stopped.

Rachel placed her hand, on his shoulder and stated, "Oh no, your going to tell me more than that, I want to know everything about you." Ralph said, "I worked hard in school and set my life's goal, to be a plastic surgeon and I am here working with Dr. Edward Kennedy the most renown plastic surgeon in the world, for my internship."

Rachel asks, "Ralph what made you think about, becoming a plastic surgeon?" Ralph did not want to tell her about Rolf, he had kept the secret so long; he just could not talk about it, so he became silent. They walked for a while together and enjoyed the view and looking at the beautiful Paris lights of the city.

When it was time to go home they both found it hard to leave, but left with a feeling, of knowing this was the beginning of a good thing, as they kissed good-night. When Ralph arrived home in his hotel room; he began writing Rolf a letter and for the first time in his life, he could not bring himself to tell Rolf everything.

He felt guilty, for falling in love and Rolf, not able to even leave their home. He wrote the letter, but did not tell Rolf, about Rachel. He did not know what to do, he thought, "Should I tell Rachel or Rolf about each other, but the answer was NO." He wrote Rolf about working at the hospital with Dr. Kennedy and even sent video's of the surgeries that was preformed by Dr. Kennedy and himself, so Rolf could learn from them.

One day Ralph and Rachel were walking around the fountain, in the park; he gave Rachel a penny and said, "Throw it in for luck." However, Rachel stood on the curve to throw the penny in, when her foot slipped and she fell in the water and began laughing, "Ha, Ha." He reached out his hand to help her out of the water and she pulled him in the water with her and they both began to laugh, "Ha, Ha, Ha."

They looked up, when they heard a policeman saying, "No one is allowed in the water and you two must get out" he smiled, as he walked away and they were laughing, "Ha, Ha" as they helped, each other out and went home. They spent every possible moment together, that they could between studies and working.

They went on boat rides, at night and listen to the Paris beautiful music and watched the lights, of the stars and the city. It became harder and harder, for Ralph to find the words enough for a letter to Rolf, so they became shorter letters. Therefore, the letters coming back to Ralph, from Rolf were filled with frustration and anger asking, "Why are your letters so short and when are you coming home?"

Ralph tried to help Rolf to understand the time it takes to do internship training under Dr. Kennedy. However, Rolf would not stop with the angry words in his letters and e-mails. Nevertheless, Ralph continued to tell Rolf that he loved him and it was going to take time, trying to reassure him.

In the mean time, Ralph and Rachel were falling deeper in love, as time went by. They spent their time walking, talking, riding bikes and boat rides, through the city and just holding each other, but both agreed that they would save themselves for marriage. One day while working, Ralph asks Dr. Kennedy, "Edward I would like to propose to Rachel, do you have any suggestions, where I could buy her engagement ring?"

Dr. Kennedy was smiling as he replied, "Congratulations Ralph, I would recommend Maxim's. So that very afternoon, he stopped in Maxim's. The shop was filled with elegance pieces of jewelry from around the world. However, after looking for a while, he came across an antique engagement two carrot diamond ring he purchased that just seemed right for Rachel.

Ralph then began making plans for Friday evening for his proposal of marriage. He phoned Rachel asking, "Darling, would you meet me at my hotel, Friday evening about seven?" She giggled softly as she said, "Of course dear." However, Friday evening when she arrives, he meets Rachel outside the hotel.

Rachel is wondering "Why is he standing outside with a bouquet of flowers" but does not say a word, as He looks at her, takes her hand, and leads her down the street to Rue de Buci, bought a bottle of champagne.

Rachel, filled with curiosity looked up into Ralph's eyes, smiling as she asks, "Honey what are you up to?"

He just looked down, at her and smiled saying, "Trust me" as they walked to the pier to board the Bat obus to tour Paris by boat. When they entered the boat, a man stepped up and said, "This way please" leading them to a small table in the center, with candles lit and a very nice dinner, prepared for two.

Rachel asks again, "Honey, what does all this mean?" Ralph smiled as he pulled out her chair for her to sit down. Then he got on one knee, took her by the hand and asks, "Rachel my love, will you please marry me?" Excitedly, she wrapped her arms around his neck and shouted, "Yes, Yes, Yes."

He, then took the ring out of his pocket and placed it on her finger, she giggled, as she shouted, "Oh Ralph, I love it" as she was looking at the, diamonds glistening in the moon light. They toured Paris by boat, in each others arms, while drinking champagne, laughing and talking all the night through.

The next morning, they had breakfast at the restaurant Du Pre. Still filled with excitement, Rachel said, "Let's go right now, to call your parents" He lingered for awhile then, he replied, "I think it would be better for me to write a letter, to my parents." She smiled and never questioned his decision, reaching her hand across the table, holding his hand.

Still smiling and taking him by the hand, as to lift him from his chair she said, "Well we can call my mother" smiling back at her, he replied, "Splendid, my dear" as he was getting out of his chair, to follow her to the phone. Rachel called her mother and began telling her, all about Ralph.

Rachel said, "Oh mother he is wonderful, he is from Atlanta, Georgia, he is six-foot three inches tall, muscular build, he is finishing his internship to become a plastic surgeon." She continued telling her mother about his parents saying, "His father Ralph Chamberlain, is the owner of, the Chamberlain Computer Company and his mother Victoria, is the social queen, of Atlanta."

Finally, Rachel said, "Mother we are engaged" paused "However, we are going to wait, until our careers are up and going before we are married." Ruth was a bit overwhelmed, with so much information at one time replied, "Well let me speak to my future son-in-law." Rachel gave the phone to Ralph, and he said, "Hello, Ruth I know we haven't met, but I feel as though I know you, through Rachel talking about you excessively."

She replied, "I would like to say the same, but for some reason my daughter has not mentioned you, once to me" Ralph turned to look at Rachel, as he wondered, why she had not mentioned him to her mother. Ruth continued, "Ralph I would like to meet you and your family, so we can become as one family, that's how it works in the family I grew up in and I would like to continue that tradition."

Ralph said, "When we come back to the states, I promise we will all meet together." Ruth then asks, "Ralph have you ever been to Oklahoma and of course he said, "No I haven't, but I certainly look forward to it." Then she asks, "Ralph do you have a large family, do you have any brothers or sisters?"

There was a long pause, before Ralph answered, "Ruth it was nice speaking with you and we will call you again soon, here is Rachel" as he was handing the phone back to her. Rachel said, "Mother we need to go for now, talk to you soon" Ruth replied, "Wait Rachel why couldn't he answer my question?"

Rachel asks, "What, question Mom?" She said, "I ask him if he had any brothers or sisters but he would not answer me, why?" Rachel took a deep breath and said, "Mom if he had any brothers or sisters, he would have already told me before now, because we have been together a year."

Ruth replied, "You need to find out why, he is keeping secrets, before you continue this relationship any further." Rachel was not going to let her mother ruin the moment, so she said, "Mom we have to go, we have a lot to do before tomorrow, we love you." She hung up the phone turned to Ralph and said, "Well, what you think of my, Mom?"

As he was drinking his coffee he said, "I think she is great and I can't wait to meet her" although he was relieved, the questions were over.

Ralph was still wondering why, Rachel did not tell her mother about their relationship before now; but, was not about to question her about it, because after all she may turn the question back at him; and she may want to know his secret, so he left that thought alone.

As they were walking and holding hands, they began talking about plans for their lives together, after they are married. Ralph said, "I am going home and write my parents tonight and I will see you tomorrow" as he kissed her goodnight. However, when he starting writing the letter he was thinking about Rolf so this is what he wrote.

The Letter

Dear Father and Mother,

I have some great news, to tell you however, I do not want Rolf to find out until, I can tell him myself. I met a girl by the name of, Rachel Royal she is from Lawton, Oklahoma. We have fallen in love and we are now, engaged. Her father was Daniel Royal a railroad engineer however; he was killed in a train wreck, when Rachel was only eight years old.

Her mother's name is Ruth Royal, a bookkeeper for a restaurant, in Lawton. Rachel has been going to college in Paris, to be a chef and when she returns home, she wants to open her own restaurant. We both are coming home to the states, I in Atlanta and she in Lawton. After a time we will marry and I hope we will have your, blessing.

Inside I have placed some copies of the photos taken, as we visited different sites' of Paris. Isn't Rachel beautiful, with her long blonde hair and sky blue eyes?" When we return to the states I will set up a time, to bring Rachel, by to meet you. I will go for now, but I will write back soon.

Love, Your Son Ralph II

When Ralph finished the letter to his parents, he then began writing a letter to Rolf, but the words would not come to him. Nevertheless,

Ralph wrote to Rolf about the things, he had always written that someday they would be together, in the world. Ralph also, told Rolf that he would be home in six months.

However, the next time they were together hugging Ralph tried to make an advance, by kissing her neck and began, to kiss to close to her breast. Rachel pulled away snapping at him, "Ralph I know we have already discussed this, but I hope you understand that, I am saving myself for marriage, because it is the right thing to do and that is the way I was raised."

Ralph quickly said, "I am sorry, of course I understand, it is hard sometimes to wait, but I understand and I will respect your decision."

Rachel said, "I love you and it is hard for me too, but we are going to wait." For the next six months, they spent every precious moment together that is the moments in between studies and working.

One day as they were walking, Rachel looked at Ralph saying, "You know dear, there is not one thing that you do not know about me, my heart is completely open to you, but I feel that you are holding something back from me." Shocked, that she knew him that well, he said, "Honey I am sorry, but I can not tell you my secret, I made a promise to myself, along time ago and I simply have to keep it for now."

She began to cry, as she said, "I hope someday you can come to trust me, as I trust you." Ralph said, "But my secret has nothing to do with trusting or not trusting. It is, just something that I have to keep to myself for now, please try to understand." She said, "I know that when you know me like I know you, then you will tell me."

He smiled, as he picked her up in the air, swung her around as he said, "You are the love of my life, my soul mate and my future bride." Rachel felt as though she would burst into tears of happiness, as they kissed. They were so happy. However, Ralph was still having a hard time letting go of Rolf while he was enjoying all this happiness.

Nevertheless time was slipping away from them, as it came time to go home. The reality, of their separation began to set in and an overwhelming sadness came over them, as they knew for a while at least, they would have to be apart. Ralph held Rachel in his arms saying, "I will go back and rush to get my career going, so we can be together" as he held her tight.

The hospital staff, Dr. Kennedy and all the other friends had a going away party for them, because Ralph was leaving for home in just three days. Then Rachel was leaving for home in two weeks. So the party took place at the Du Pre restaurant, with all their friends with dinner and dancing.

Then finally, it was time for Rachel to take Ralph to the airport, to catch his plane. Looking down into her sky blue eyes, He said, "Honey this is harder to leave you, than it was to leave" he gasped for breath, because he almost said; "Rolf" but he changed it to "my parents." She began to cry saying, "I love you with all my heart" they embraced kissing each other good-bye and he boarded the plane for home...........

RALPH COMES HOME
CHAPTER 5

R alph is still on the plane nervously, trying to make notes on how he is going to greet Rolf, when he sees him for the first time, without him knowing that he is keeping a secret from him. He knew how close, they had always been and how they understood each other. However, they have now been separated for two years nevertheless, they are still identical twins and all these thoughts are racing through his mind.

He was excited about seeing his parents, but apprehensive about seeing Rolf. The plane finally, landed in the Atlanta airport and as he walked into the waiting area, he saw his excited parents, smiling and awaiting his arrival. Victoria hugged him, as she whispered in his ear, "I am excited about your engagement to Rachel, I had her family checked out and it is a lovely family."

Shocked, Ralph stopped and snapped at her, "Mother what do you mean, you had her family checked out, and how could you do such a thing!" His father Ralph, hugged him, saying, "Ralph you know, how your mother is, she just wants the best for you." Ralph declared, to his mother, "If you do anything to cause Rachel and me any problems, I will leave and never come back."

Victoria shrugged her shoulders and replied, "I would never do anything to cause you two problems, because your father and I are very happy for you two, now lets' go home." On the way home Ralph talked excessively, about Rachel. Ralph and Victoria were so happy to see their son filled with, so much happiness.

However, when they arrived home, he began to shudder at the thought of seeing Rolf, face to face again. As he was looking up, at the stairs Victoria said, "You don't have to go up there you know." Ralph turned and looked at both of them saying, "Yes I do, I love him, but at the same time I feel guilty for being so happy, when he can't be."

His father said, "Go ahead, he is waiting to see you too, we will be here, when you come down, then we can all sit down for a nice family dinner together." So Ralph ran upstairs, opened the sound proof door, then closing it behind him, ran into the den where the TV was playing, Rolf jumped up, when he saw Ralph and they embraced with tears of happiness.

Ralph talked and Rolf signed about all that they had learned over the past two years however, Rolf could tell something was different, about his brother. Rolf looked at Ralph, with a serious look, signing, "What is going on, Ralph something is different about you, I can tell, you are keeping a secret from me."

Ralph trying to reassure him, said, "No Rolf, you are mistaken; I am just trying to get readjusted to home." Later, Ralph stated, "Rolf, I have to go downstairs to unpack, but I will see you tomorrow." Rolf took Ralph's arm saying, "Please don't go, I missed you to much" but, Ralph pulled away as he said, "I will be back, I promise."

However, when he came downstairs, his parents were waiting, to have dinner with him. While they were eating, Victoria said, "My dear, we have decided to have an engagement party for you and Rachel." Ralph spoke up, "I would prefer the party to wait until, and Rolf can join us." Victoria shouted, "Well, that will never happen in this home, I will assure you of that."

His father, Ralph said, "Son, why don't you focus on having an engagement party with us and later you can have another party with Rolf" looking at Ralph, hoping to keep peace in the family. Ralph stated, "It doesn't matter, what we do now, but I am telling both of you, that Rolf is going to someday be apart of this family or you two will lose, both of us" as he threw his napkin on the floor and walked out of the room.

Nevertheless, Victoria had an engagement party for Ralph and Rachel. Rachel's mother, Ruth came as well as their friends and family on both sides. After the party, Ralph took Rachel by the hand as they walked around the plantation. Ralph saddled two horses, from the stable while asking Rachel, "Pet will you please, go for a ride with me?" She replied, "Certainly, darling" as she climbed on the horse.

As they were riding, Ralph asks Rachel a strange thing. He asks, "Rachel, I know this will seem to be strange to you, but I am going to ask that you trust me." She looked at him, with confusion as she asks, "Why are you asking me to trust you, when you know that I trust you with all of my heart."

Smiling at her, Ralph said, "Yes, I know Pet, but now I ask, that you trust me with this request that I have; I am asking that you not come back to see me again, until I have finished my task." The horses were walking along the creek, trying to drink the water, but Ralph said, "You can't let them drink now; they have to wait until we get back to the stables."

Rachel looking at him with tears, coming down her cheeks asks, "Why can't I come back to see you?" Ralph stopped his horse and took her off her horse, and wrapped his arms around her. Then he said, "Oh, my darling, I did not mean you could never come back." She said, "But, what is your task, that is stopping us from seeing each other."

Ralph said, "Pet, do you remember that you asks me, if I had a secret that I could not tell you?" She said, "Yes" looking up at him waiting for him to tell her his secret." He looked at her with a serious look, as he said, "I can't tell you my secret yet, but if you will trust me and give me two years; I promise, I will tell you everything and we can be married and I will never keep another secret from you, as long as I live."

Rachel began to cry as she asks, "Two years, why do you need so long, for this task of yours?" He took her face with his hands making her look at him as he said, "Rachel, do you believe that I love you, with all of my heart?" She could tell that he was sincere, she said, "Yes, I believe you love me, but why so long?"

He said, "If you will wait, for me, I promise, you will understand in the end; I promise, we can talk on the phone everyday, but please do this for me." So she promised to stay away for two years, so he could finish his task. Ralph hugged her tightly and cried with her. As they kissed each other, she knew she could trust him.

The next morning Ralph took her to the airport and they kissed each other for the last time, well, at least for two years and Rachel boarded the plane going back home to Oklahoma. A few days later, Ralph's (father), Ralph said, "Son let's go for a drive, I want to show you something."

So Ralph, Ralph II and Victoria went for a drive, "Where are we going?" asks Ralph II. Victoria replied, "Oh no, it is a surprise and you will find out when we get there."

Ten minutes later, they drove into a driveway of a large brick building, and Victoria said, "Alright, Ralph close your eyes" as she came around the car and opened the door and led him into the building. Ralph II asks, "What is all of this, what are you two up to now?" Ralph said, "Son open you eyes and take a look around your new office building."

Ralph II began shouting, "You have got to be kidding, is this for real?" as he hugged his mother and father shouting, "Thank-you, Thank-you, now I can fix Rolf's face as soon as possible." Victoria threw her hand on her hip shouting, "Oh no, that is not why we have you this building, this is for your practice, not for Rolf."

Ralph II did not dare say Rolf's name again, but kept his plans to himself. Victoria stated, "Ralph II, your father and I will get what ever you need to make this place your plastic surgery hospital, so let's get to work." So the three of them made the building a place to talk about; and it only took two months from start to finish.

The place was decorated, by the best in the field for small hospitals, with the best equipment. Ralph hired his staff and now was ready for Rolf.....

THE SURGERY
CHAPTER 6

The day finally came, Ralph had made sure everyone was gone from their home, he walked upstairs unlocked the sound proof door and Ralph and Rolf walked out of the home together, for the first time. For the first time in Rolf's life since he was brought home from the hospital, he was leaving home.

However, when he walked down stairs he stopped, looked around. Standing on the staircase, looking at the rooms downstairs and signed, "Ralph was all this here all the time?" "Yes it has always been just like this" answered Ralph. Unknowing to Ralph, Rolf was harboring all these things in his heart, that he had been deprived; as he was looking at the family photos on the way downstairs.

As they walked outside, it became overwhelming; to Rolf he had to sit down on the steps, because he was having a panic attack.

Ralph asks, "Rolf just sit here for awhile, what is wrong?" he signed, "don't you understand, I have never seen the real sky, real grass or anything outside of the prison of the upstairs of this house, I hate everyone that allowed this to happen to me." He reached down and touched the grass for the first time, seeing bugs; he saw a butterfly flying around the flowers full of color.

Then he looked at the sky for along time signing, "Is the sky always this blue" Ralph replied, "I have never really thought about it, but I guess it is beautiful." Rolf turned and looked at him with anger signing,

"You have always seen these things, but I haven't and it is not fair" Ralph replied, "I agree that is why I became a plastic surgeon" Rolf signed, "This is so much better than seeing it on TV or in books."

Then, as the wind was blowing, looking at his brother, with a puzzled look on his face, Rolf stopped, as he was holding his face with one hand; as he signed, with the other, "What is this I feel on my face, my arms and hands." Ralph stopped, as he was trying to understand what, Rolf was signing about, when he realized, he said, "Rolf that is the wind."

Rolf watched with amazement, as a soft breeze was blowing the leaves of the trees. Guilt, gripped Ralph's heart, as he watched Rolf taking in real life, for the first time. He thought about his parents and everything they had depraved Rolf and now he is seeing the outside world, as this grand tour anew and it was all unnecessary, because of their pride.

Ralph said, "Take your time, I will wait" "No, I am ready to start my new life" as Rolf walked to the car, slowly across the grass, for the first time, because it was a different feeling under his feet. But, now another new experience, he had never ridden in a car since he was brought home, after his birth. So he slowly got in the car "We will go slowly, don't be afraid" said, Ralph, realizing all the things he had taken for granted, was all so new to Rolf.

Ralph felt bad, that it had taken so long for Rolf to be able to leave home Rolf had been building resentment up more and more in his heart.

On the way to Ralph's building, Rolf noticed everything, people walking along the streets, a dog chasing a cat, children playing on the play ground.

He saw, construction workers remodeling the front of a house, people smoking, and an old lady sitting on her front porch, rocking back and forth, as Ruby used to do in his room. It was so overwhelming, he signed in Ralph's face, "I am going to be sick" Ralph stopped the car, Rolf got out and vomited; then looking distressed he signed, "This is to much for me, I just can't take it all in".

Ralph realizing what had happened, that Rolf was seeing to much, to fast replied, "Rolf lay down in the back seat; don't try to take in anymore today, because you have the rest of your life to see it all." So he did. When they arrived at Ralph's building, he drove to the back door, got out walked around the car, opened the door for Rolf and said, "Rolf just close your eyes and I will led you to your room."

Rolf signed, "No, I will follow you I am free and no more doors will be locked." Ralph smiled at him as he said, "No Rolf, I didn't mean it that way, I just didn't want you to get sick again." Then they walked into the area Rolf where would be staying. They walked into the bedroom. As Rolf got closer to the far wall, he saw a picture of Ralph hanging on the wall, turned to Ralph signing, "After my surgery, our photo will be hanging here" Ralph smiled, "You are right."

Then they saw the bathroom and small kitchen area. Rolf was surprised, to see such a small place he signed, "Why is my home, so small" looking angry. Ralph wanted to reassure him, he said, "No, Rolf this is not your home, this is only temporary, only until we make your face like everyone else. Remember, I explained this before, this is not a home, but a hospital to help you."

He signed, "I want to see the rest of your building" Ralph stated, "I think you have had enough excitement for one day, don't you? Can you wait until the morning?" Rolf looking a bit apprehensive, signed, "Where are you going to stay, I only see one bed?" "I am going back home, but you will be alright here and I will see you in the morning, just take it easy and rest" as he laid Rolf's bag on the bed and left.

After Ralph walked out, Rolf turned the knob on the door to make sure it wasn't locked; Ralph smiled, when he heard it, because he knew what, Rolf was doing. After an hour of resting, he was feeling better. He then decided to explore the hospital. He walked down the hall, thinking he was alone in the hospital.

Rolf entered another room; suddenly he was startled, seeing a man lying in bed, with his head wrapped in bandages. The man asks, "Do you work here or are you a patient?" Rolf turned quickly, to walk out, but the man said, "Please don't go you are the first person to come see me since I came here."

Rolf walked back over to the bed and signed, "What happened to you? Why are you here?" The man said, "I can't understand sign language, but let me guest, you are here for your surgery and you want to know what happened to me?" Rolf shook his head, up and down, to let the man know, he was right.

Looking through the bandages, with only one eye and his mouth exposed, the man said, "Well let me tell you what happened to me, I had a fight with my wife and I ran out of my house filled with rage, got in my car and drove it straight into a tree, without a seatbelt and I went threw the windshield."

Rolf became angry, when he realized the man did that to himself and knowing that he did not have a choice, about his deformity so he left the room. He yelled, "Wait come back, where are you going?" Rolf would not even look back at the man. He then began walking, down the hall seeing the hospital, comparing it with the entire photos Ralph had given him; it was well equipped as the pictures Ralph had showed him.

Then he saw the nurse's station, the nurse sitting at her desk looked at him and smiled, but afraid to say anything, he started to walk away. She said, "Wait you must be Rolf, are you lost" he looked puzzled, that she knew him, he signed, "No I just want to look around, but how did you know my name?"

She smiled, "We all know, who you are and we have been waiting for you, would you like for me, to show you around" holding her hand out to him. This was the first time that he felt at ease and began to feel that he was going to be alright in the outside world. He signed; "Yes" she took him by the hand and led him around the hospital describing each room to him.

She began, "This is a small hospital, having only ten inpatient rooms, an operating room, and a recovery room; however your brother Ralph wanted you to have the best place in this hospital that is why you are in his space." Rolf looked surprised that Ralph had given him the best, even his own space he signed, "I am happy to be here" "I am glad you are here too. By the way, my name is Judy Philman" as she smiled at him.

The next morning Ralph came walking into Rolf's room, saying, "Now we can get down to business" as he was holding two cups of coffee, offering one cup to Rolf. Rolf took the cup of coffee and signed, "I have been ready for this for a long time, when do we start?" Ralph replied, "In the morning we will do the surgery, it should take about eight hours" Ralph spent the day with Rolf. The next morning……..

Dr. Kennedy had flown over to assist in the surgery. The surgery was underway and it did take eight hours as Ralph had predicted. Two days later… Rolf was signing to Ralph, "Was the surgery a success?" Ralph smiled, "Yes Rolf, it is all taken care of and the bandages can come off in two weeks." Two weeks later…. The bandages were removed, Ralph gave Rolf the mirror.

When Rolf looked at himself, he gashed because he looked identical to Ralph. They both cried for joy, but sadly, Dr. Kennedy was not there for the removal of the bandages, because he had flown back home the day after the surgery had taken place. For the next two years, during this time of healing and speech therapy Rolf learned hands on surgery with Ralph. Rolf then received his degree for plastic surgery.

Rolf learned to drive and live in the world as an independent person. After awhile even his staff could not tell them apart. However, Ralph reminded his staff that Rolf and Rachel was not to know anything about each other until he could tell them. Rolf and Ralph had many conversations over the two years of Rolf's recovery from his surgery, speech therapy and his ordeal of being a prisoner in his own home.

So Ralph felt that it was time for Rolf to hear about Rachel. One afternoon Ralph walked into the room with Rolf and said, "Rolf please have a seat, I have some news to tell you." As Rolf was sitting down he said, "Well this sounds serious!" Ralph poured them a cup of coffee and when he was standing beside Rolf, he stated, "Rolf you know all my life I have tried to live solely for you" as he was trying to smile.

Ralph continued, "My thoughts were about you continually and you are the sole reason for me, becoming a plastic surgeon."

Rolf said, "Yes, and I am grateful, so what is the problem?" as he looked at Ralph with confusion. Ralph continued, "Now that you have your surgery and therapy behind you, a complete education with a license to do plastic surgery, good looks and a great future ahead of you, I feel that I can tell you my secret."

Rolf looked shocked, as he shouted, "Why did you feel that you had to keep a secret from me?" as he stood up. Ralph said, "Because I did not think it would be fair to you if I had a life and you could not, but now we both have a future." Rolf shouted, "Say on!" as he looked angry at Ralph. Ralph smiled greatly as he said, "While I was in Paris, I met a girl, her name is Rachel, we fell in love and now we are engaged."

However, the news was too overwhelming for Rolf, his head was spinning as the words, (fell in love and engaged) were played repeatedly in his head. He felt betrayed, by the only one he had trusted in his life. This was the end of the life they knew as friends and brothers.

Rolf became insanely jealous of the life Ralph had and he did not. Any thoughts of rational thinking, was gone from his mind. Out of the corner of his eye, he saw a statue on the desk, picked it up and to hit Ralph. Ralph threw up his arms, to protect himself, but it was too late, he was hit on the head and fell to the floor.

Rolf thought he had killed his brother; he became afraid and confused, not knowing what to do next. He looked through the building and everyone had gone to the front of the building for the night. He thought, "Anytime I have had a problem, I could talk it over with my brother, but now I am alone."

He went outside, brought the car around back, and began to drag Ralph, however, Ralph began to groan and cough as he was becoming conscious. Rolf was afraid to face what he had done at that point, so he grabbed the phone cord and tied Ralph up. Ralph tried to reason with Rolf, saying "Rolf listen to me, I did not betray you, and I only wanted to wait until you could" Rolf stopped him before he could finish talking and would not listen to him.

Rolf threw him into the car; Ralph was pleading with him to stop, so Rolf went back inside, grabbed some tape and tapped Ralph's mouth. Looking hardness at Ralph, he stated, "I am glad you are not dead, because now you will find out how it feels to be betrayed!" Ralph lay in the back seat feeling helpless and wondering, "What is he going to do, is he going to kill me?"

Rolf drove into the driveway of their home, walked around the car, threw Ralph over his shoulder and carried him up to the third story of their home. He then walked into the upstairs living room, put Ralph down into a chair and securely tied him to it and removed the tape from his mouth. Ralph pleaded, "Please Rolf, tell me what you are going to do?"

Rolf looked at him, "Sure, I will tell you what I am going to do, I am going to kill Rachel!" then he turned and walked out. Ralph was screaming, "Please Rolf, you can't hurt her, she has never done anything to you." Rolf walked back down stairs, found Ralph's room and began throwing things everywhere.

Then, he found the love letters and pictures from Rachel. Sitting down in the middle of the floor, Rolf begins to read each letter and look at the photos one by one. After reading some of the letters he realized, Rachel did not know about him either, he raged inside thinking, "Ralph must have been ashamed of me too, all along."

He read some more, even found pictures of Rachel and Ralph with their parents, in this very house. He was thinking, "They had, had parties in this very house with me just upstairs and left me out of everything, betrayed and unloved." He then began to make a plan, how he could hurt them like they hurt him."

Then, he immediately made plane reservations, for that evening to fly to Oklahoma. He got Rachel's phone number from her from the love letters, immediately called Rachel, pretending to be Ralph and said, "Rachel, I am flying out to see you tonight, can you pick me up at the airport?" Excitement in her voice, "Of course I can, darling."

Rolf went to Ralph's room and packs a bag. He then went back upstairs, sat a chair. In front of the chair, Ralph is sitting and says, "Pretending to be you, I called the love of your life, she will meet me at the airport in Oklahoma tonight and then I will kill her." Ralph begged, cried and screamed, "Please don't hurt her, she doesn't even know you, please don't hurt her!"

Rolf looked at him and said, "That is why, you were ashamed of me and could not tell her about me." Ralph shouted, "No, you are taking everything wrong, I only wanted to protect your feelings." Rolf walked out, closed the sound proof door behind him. Ralph felt helpless and alone with thoughts of Rolf killing his beloved.

Rolf got to the airport, boarded the plane and thought of different ways he could kill Rachel.......

THE RAPE
CHAPTER 7

Wh ile Rolf was on the plane, all these things were replaying through his mind, burning into his memory, how he had watched Ralph's smile and heard him saying, "Rachel is the love of my life and we are getting married and I would like" and how he knew, he had to stop Ralph, because he could not stand to hear anymore, he stopped him, before he could finish speaking.

Rolf felt betrayed by his brother. Inside Rolf had hit a boiling point. His memory replaying how, he had reached and found a weapon which happened to be a small statue on the desk, hitting him on the head and Ralph fell to the floor. He cringed as he thought back, that he could have killed Ralph and glad that he did not.

Rolf replayed in his mind when, Ralph asks, "Are you going to kill me?" he was replaying his thoughts "No I have something better in mine", as he smirked. His last replay in his mind of his last words to Ralph, he shouted, "I am going to kill Rachel and I will come back to tell you all about it."

When Rolf arrived at the airport, he began walking toward the baggage claim, when he saw Rachel running to meet him. She ran to Rolf throwing her arms around his neck saying, "I love you with all my heart." When Rachel hugged Rolf, he decided at that very moment to keep her for himself.

He wrapped his arms around her beautiful soft small framed

body, falling in love with her at once. He thought about how Ralph must have felt, as he must have heard those words many times from her and his parents; knowing he was not cared for at all. The jealousy arose within him.

For his best revenge he decided, to marry her himself. In his mind, he felt that if he married her, he could make her fall in love with him instead, of Ralph then tell her that he was Ralph's twin brother Rolf. He remembered in her letters that Ralph called, her "Pet" so he said, and "Pet, let's go get married today."

Stunned, she looked up at him and said, "Honey, please come home with me, I want you to see mother, she has been waiting to see you again." Rolf trying not to show his quick temper replied, "We will have plenty of time to see her afterwards" as his eyes firmly locked to hers as not to give her a choice in the matter.

Rachel backed up looking at him, thinking this is the first time I remember Ralph being so forceful, she was feeling uneasy for the first time in their relationship. However, Rachel shrugged her shoulders and put it out of her mind. She was so happy to see him she shouted, with excitement, "Yes, I will marry you today."

They picked up Rolf's (Ralph's) luggage and went shopping, Rachel picked out a beautiful white dress and he bought a black suit. They bought a camera on the way to the court house. As they arrived at the courthouse, in Lawton, Oklahoma and still in the car Rachel looked at him and ask, "Honey, do you really love me?" "Yes" Rolf said nervously.

"Very well let's get married" said Rachel with excitement. The wedding ceremony was sweet, an elderly couple named Mr. and Mrs. Mims, stood as the witnesses, as the judge announced them as Mr. and Mrs. Ralph (Rolf) Chamberlain. So they were married October 23, 1987. Not knowing how to behave around a woman, because he had never been taught, Rolf looked at her and said, "Pet let's go straight to the hotel."

Rachel felt a bit strange, because of Ralph's (Rolf's) behavior but shrugged it off for the second time, she replied, "No honey, I agreed to get married today, but it would not be fair to leave my mother waiting and not knowing what is going on and I just can not tell her on the phone" Rolf reluctantly agreed.

On the way she said, "Honey, I am so happy and mother already loves you, I can't wait to see her face when we tell her." Rolf did not say a word all the way to Rachel's mother's house. When they arrived Rachel opened the door and they walked inside. Her mother came into the room and Rachel smiled from ear to ear, as she said, "Ralph (Rolf) this is my mother Ruth Royal and Mother this is my husband Ralph (Rolf) Chamberlain."

With a Shocked look on her face Ruth said, "Husband, what do, you mean?" Rachel said, "Yes, mother we just came from the courthouse where we were married, I know that is not what we discussed, but we wanted to get married today, so we did." Ruth said, "Well, I have made some tea sit down and we can talk for awhile before you go." "No, we are leaving for the hotel now" shouted Rolf.

Ruth asks with concern for her daughter in her voice, "Rachel could I speak with you in the kitchen for a moment, Please?" So they stepped into the kitchen and Ruth said, "Rachel this man does not seem to be the same man you have spoken so often or the man that I met in Georgia and has spoken with me so often on the phone."

Rachel being so much in love, did not listen to her mother's warning or the feeling, she herself had deep inside telling her, this is the wrong man. She said to her mother, "Everything will be alright mother, you will see." Rachel said, "Mother I think we need to go, but I will call you tomorrow love you."

They walked back into the living room and Rachel said to Ralph (Rolf), "Honey, lets go to a restaurant and eat before going to the hotel, I know a great place" Rolf said, "Let's go" as they were walking out, Rolf looked back at Ruth with a blank stare. Ruth felt the hair stand up on her arms and a strange feeling came over her as she watched them leave.

Later they arrived at the hotel and as they entered the room, Rolf locked the door. As he did his disposition changed again. Rachel turned to look at Ralph (Rolf) to see the change in his eyes with that blank stare, her mother had seen and a fear came over her, because of his strange behavior. As he began walking slowly toward her, she said, "Ralph stop staring at me like that, you are frightening me."

Rolf grabbed her by her arms, enabling her from moving away from him. She looked up at him crying and begging, "Please Ralph, let me go, this is not the way to treat your new bride." He was not listening to her, he picked her up threw her on the bed and started ripping off her blouse. "Please Ralph, you know I am still a virgin, Please be easy with me, I saved myself for you," she screamed.

Rolf was still not listening to her; she is so confused about the actions her new husband has taken against her. All the while she was screaming and begging, "Please stop, not like this Please stop, stop" tears flowing from her eyes. He reached over grabbed the phone cord, snatched it out of the wall, cut in half and tied each of her arms to a bed post.

He then walked into the bathroom and ripped out that phone cord, came back and tied her legs, one each of the bottom bed post. Then he ripped off her shoes, and the rest of her clothes. He touched and kissed her slowly. She is still crying and begging. Rolf then stands up and takes off his clothes and finishes raping her, taking away her virginity.

Rachel was exhausted, as her voice was weak she begged, "Ralph please give me some clothes out of my bag or at the very least cover me, please." Rolf got up and stared at her laying there a small soft delicate blonde beautiful light skin, thinking to himself, how beautiful she is. However, he would not let her have her clothes but he gently covered her with a blanket.

She looked at him and asks, "Ralph what are you going to do with me now, are you going to kill me?" He said, "No, I just wanted to make you mine." She shouted, "That is not the way to make me yours, you are supposed to be gentle and kind, what has happened to you?" Rolf looked at her and said, "I really love you, I really do." She cried, "This is not love, this is control."

He went to the bathroom and drew bath water for her and walked back into the room untied her, gently picked her up, walked into the bathroom put her in the tub and gently gave her a bath. Rachel was afraid to fight, so she just lay there and let him have control, because she did not know what he would do to her, if she fought with him.

After he gave her a bath, he carried her back into the bedroom, laid her on the bed. He then began to repeat his process tying her arms and legs in the same position, as before. She begged, "Please let me go I won't tell anyone about this, but please, let me go" "No, I'll never let you go, I love you" he shouted and smiled at her.

Rolf lay by her side, as he continued to rub and play with her most of the night and raping her again and again. The next morning he got up and left the room, leaving a do not disturb sign on the outside of the door. Rachel screamed for help, to no avail. Later, Rolf came back with breakfast saying, "Pet, I brought us something to eat."

Rachel shouted, "Don't ever call me Pet again, you have hurt me. Don't you understand that" looking at him, to see if just maybe he understood anything she was saying. Rolf said, "Pet, we are not leaving this hotel, until you calm down and realize that I love you and you love me, is that understood!" looking firm into her eyes, with his eyes glazed.

Rachel realized, she had to play the game until, she could convince him that very thing was alright, if she wanted to be free of him. She said, "Ok honey, can I have my clothes now" No, not today, but tomorrow, because today will be our day. Rolf repeated his slow rape of her over again. Rachel cried and begged again, until she was so exhausted, she could do nothing but just lay there and he did what ever he wanted to her, all that day too.

The next morning, Rolf woke up his hand still lying on her breast, he kisses both her breast, and got up from beside her, untied her arms and legs. Then he picked her up, carried her back to the tub, climbed in with her and gave them both a bath. Afterward, he dressed her saying, "Now lets' go visit your mother" Rachel looked at him strangely, thinking; now he thinks everything is going to be as it was before.

Rachel was afraid to say anything on the way to her mother's for fear he may turn around and rape her again. However, still not sure that he really was going to take her to her mothers' until they actually arrived. Once they arrived she ran inside, but did not make a scene for fear he may hurt both, her and her mother.

Rachel asks, "Mother may I speak with you in the next room" Ruth could sense that something was wrong as she said, "Of course dear." Once they were in the kitchen Rachel began to cry, "Mother he raped me" Ruth ran back into the living room with Rachel behind her and yelled, "Why did you rape my daughter."

Rolf said, "What are you talking about, I love your daughter, now stop all of this nonsense. Rachel pack your bags, you are going home with me to live in our home in Georgia today." Rachel knew she had to be careful with what she said, for the fear of what he may do, "Ralph you go on ahead and I will pack and join you later, there is just too much to do in one day" as she trembled.

Her mother watching realized, what she was doing, said, "Yes, Ralph you go on ahead, I will help her pack." Rolf surprisingly said, "Alright Pet, I love you and I will see you soon" as he turned and walked out of the door. After Rolf left, Ruth shouted, "Now we have to call the police and get you to a doctor."

Rachel began to cry bitterly saying, "No, mother please I just need to rest, please I just can't tell anyone about this." Ruth realized, Rachel had been brutally raped and did not want to make her go through anymore at this time; agreed to let her alone for the time being. Rachel ran to her room at laid across her bed and cried until she went to sleep.

Ruth called in to both their jobs saying, "We are sick and will be staying home for a few days" as she sat down in the living room and cried herself to sleep also. Ruth stayed home to comfort Rachel, as best she could not knowing what was going to happen next; because of the change in Ralph (Rolf) fear gripped, them both, that he may return.........

THE MURDER
CHAPTER 8

━━━∾⁓∾━━━

Later, after Rolf had arrived home and made sure Ralph had food and water. Ralph begged him, "Please tell me that Rachel is alright?" Rolf said, "Oh, she is better than alright, we were married two days ago." Ralph shouted, "That is impossible, Rachel could not be fooled by you, she knows me all to well." Rolf said, "Don't flatter yourself, she thinks that you raped her and enjoyed it" with tears flowing down his cheeks, Ralph shouted, "You raped her?"

Rolf walking away from him stated, "Yes, and she is now my wife and I am keeping her, for myself and now it is our parents turn." Then Rolf walked back downstairs to wait for his parents to come home from vacation, the time has arrived. Rolf (pretending to be Ralph Jr.) smiled, as he waited to avenge himself of his parents, pacing back and fourth across the floor. Upstairs the third story door was ajar, so Ralph could hear what was happening or going to happen……..

Ralph still tied to the chair, was trying to think of away to get out of his dilemma, so he could help his parents. However, nothing comes to mind, except that he was helpless, filled with overwhelming fear, as he trembled, tears flowed down his cheeks. Then he had the horrible thought about Rolf killing his parents.

The front door opened as Victoria shouted, "Ralph dear, are you here?" Rolf smiled as he walked in saying, "Yes, Mother I am here." Rolf continued, "How was your trip" nervously watching them, hoping they would not find out his true identity "Very nice" replied, Ralph Sr...

Rolf said, "Well, I have some news for you two" Victoria watching Rolf, because he was behaving strangely, stated, "Ralph you seem so serious, is it bad news?" "No, in fact it is great news, Rachel and I got married two days ago and she is home with her mother, packing as we speak."

Victoria gashed and trembled, as she was looking into Ralph (Rolf's) eyes, she began backing up, pointing her finger at him, saying, "Something is wrong, this is just not right" as she realized that he was really Rolf. Knowing his cover was blown, his temper flared, as he angrily shouted, "If you two want to live, you will keep my secret."

Ralph Sr. trembled, as he shouted, "What have you done with your brother, Ralph, Please tell me that you have not hurt him?"

Victoria put her hands to her face as she began to scream, "Where is he what have you done with my son?" as tears flowed down her cheeks. Rolf snapped, "No I have not hurt him, but I will, if I have to. Are you going to keep my secret or not?" She shouted, "NO stay away from us you could never be like my son Ralph" trembling in fear for what he may do, she quickly backed away from him.

Ralph Sr. started walking toward him, saying, "Rolf you have not hurt anyone" but before he could finish speaking; Rolf turned, as he was still filled with rage, picked up a fire iron, from the fireplace and hit his father on the head. Then watching him fall to the floor, knowing he was dead, instantly.

But he now was filled with fear and anger, because his intention was not to kill him, but stop him. Terrified, Victoria began screaming, "Help me, somebody, help me" as she ran through the dining room, into the kitchen and out the back door. (Meanwhile upstairs Ralph was hearing everything that was going on, with tears flowing down his cheeks and completely helpless his heart, aching as it pounded heavily.)

Ralph was thinking, "This has to be a nightmare." Rolf heard the back door close, so he ran after her. Rolf's rage gave him super strength, when he caught up with her he grabbed her by the hair and drug her back into the kitchen. Victoria begged, "Please don't hurt me Please" "Did you listen as I said those very same words to you, only being five years old?" asks Rolf, as he looked wild eyed.

"I am sorry, Please don't hurt me" Victoria still begged with her lips trembling. He grinned, as a mad man, snatched the phone cord out of the wall and tied her to a chair that he had taken from the breakfast room, then grabbed duct tape from the pantry and taped her mouth, leaving her with her thoughts, as he walked back upstairs to Ralph.

As he approached Ralph trembling, with fear and grief, Ralph tried to talk however; he could not because his mouth was taped. Rolf snatched the tape off Ralph's mouth. Ralph whimpered, "Are Mom and Dad ok, please tell me?" "No they are not, Dad is dead and Mom is going to be shortly" He shouted, Rolf with eyes glazed, he was pacing back and forward in the room like a mad man.

Ralph screamed, with tears flowing down his cheeks, "Why did you kill Dad, Please don't kill Mother" Rolf turned, looking at Ralph, as he was walking away. As he was grinning, "I will leave the door open so you can hear mother screaming for her life." Ralph still screaming, over and over to no avail, "Pease don't kill mother, I will do what ever you say, but please don't kill mother."

Victoria could hear Ralph screaming and knew she was going to die. Her heart was racing, as tears flowed down her cheeks. Rolf stepped back into the kitchen, his eyes filled with rage, looking at his mother shaking and tears flowing as he said, "Remember my fear and tears." Rolf ripped off the tape from her mouth and she began to beg, "Please Rolf, I am sorry for all that I have done, I can't go back and change it, please don't kill me."

Rolf walked off and let her scream. He took a shovel from the garden shed and dug a shallow grave, in the freshly planted garden, in the back yard. Then he slowly walked back through the house, passing by his mother, listening to her constant screaming and begging for her life. Then he went back into the living room, to reassess how to take his father's body outside.

Finally, Rolf picked up his father's arms and started dragging him through the house, when he came to the kitchen, he stopped. Victoria started screaming, "Oh my God, what are you going to do with him? Please, call 911 for help! You need help, please Rolf, don't do anymore please!" He did not listen to her, he continued to drag his father outside and stopped at the grave and slowly pushed his father into it, watching him as he fell into the grave.

Victoria could see part of Rolf moving around in the backyard but could not tell exactly what was going on. Then Victoria saw him coming back and began screaming, "No, No please don't," Ralph screamed from upstairs, "please, Rolf don't hurt Mother." Rolf walked back inside, took hold of the back of his mother's chair and started dragging her outside, to the garden.

He sat her chair up, stared into her eyes and said, "You are now, just beginning to feel, what I did when you locked me away with all my fear and confusion." He then duct tapped a PVC pipe in her mouth, so she could breathe when he threw her in the grave. Victoria trembling and tears flowing, Rolf pushed her into the grave, with no compassion for her.

The chair landed with Victoria looking straight up, into his cold dead eyes. With her arms and legs tied down to the chair, her mouth taped and completely helpless, Rolf said; "Now you can watch me shovel the dirt, (which was really potting soil and pine bark) in your grave."

Rolf walked back up stairs, to tell Ralph what he had done. As he entered the room Ralph was shouting, "Please tell me that mother is ok." Rolf got in Ralph's face and shouted, "Dad is dead and Mother is buried alive, in the back yard garden." Overwhelmed, Ralph shouted, "This is just too much to bear, please, Rolf don't hurt anyone else. Please go to back yard and save mother."

Rolf looked at him and grinned with his eyes glazed like a crazy maniac, not in reality. Ralph realized, Rolf had lost all sense of reasoning and it would be no use in trying to talk to him. Rolf was walking back and forth, wringing his hands, trying to think what to do next; as he was shouting repeatedly, "I have no one, but Rachel now" "I have no one, but Rachel now" No, you don't she fell in love with me and when she finds out about you she will leave you" shouted, Ralph "She will never know" replied, Rolf.

Ralph shouted, "What are you going to do with me?" Rolf went into the kitchen that was upstairs, took a knife out of the drawer and walked back in the room with Ralph staring at him. Ralph began screaming, "Please don't kill me" Rolf slowly and firmly stated, "I want you alive to know everything that I do, now it is Rachel's turn" as he put the knife in Ralph's hand. Then Rolf said, "If you live or not is up to you" and he walked out and locked the door behind him.

Rolf walked back down stairs, called the airport and made plane reservations for a flight to Oklahoma and left the house. Meanwhile upstairs Ralph was franticly cutting the tape off of his hands. Once he was free he remembered his father telling him, there was sheetrock placed over the windows of the third floor.

He began knocking on the wall, for the hollow places to find a window. Once he found one; he took the knife and cut through it to the window. He tore off the sheetrock and opened the window. Then he took sheets, tied them together and climbed down to the ground. However, he was still afraid Rolf maybe around, so Ralph went to his car opened it and used his car phone to call 911.

The operator asked, "911, what is your emergency?" Ralph shouted, "Help me, my brother killed my father and may have killed my mother" as he was crying hysterically. The 911 operator asks, "What is your address sir?" He told them. Then he ran to the backyard, to save his mother.

However, Rolf had not left in fact; he was walking around the house, when he saw the sheets hanging down from the third story window. Rolf's rage heightens, as he realized, there had been windows up there all the time, he was growing up. Rolf began screaming, "Kill, Kill I am going to kill you."

Ralph overheard Rolf screaming, Ralph ran for his life, as he entered the front door of the house. Ralph ran back upstairs locking the door behind him. Rolf ran into the house, and then heard the door close upstairs, He ran upstairs and tired to open it, but he couldn't. Then Rolf remembered the sheets, hanging down from the window.

He ran back outside and around the house, Ralph was looking out the window waiting for the police, when they saw each other. Rolf took hold of the sheets and began to climb up and Ralph quickly grabbed the knife, he had used to free himself and began to cut the sheets. Rolf fell to the ground still filled with rage. He went to the barn grabbed an ax and then ran back into the house.

Rolf was holding the ax in his hand, as he started running back up the stairs, yelling, "I am going to kill you." The police entered the house shouting, "Stop or we will shoot!" Rolf stopped, turned and dropped the ax. The police threw him on the floor and arrested him. Then the police yelled, "This is the police, who is up there, it is alright you can come down now."

Ralph slowly opened the door, and yelled, "Is he still in the house" the police, yelled back, "No he is in the police car we have arrested him." The police where shocked, to see that Ralph was identical to the man they had just arrested. They said to Ralph, "Let's go into the kitchen and we can sit down to talk."

Ralph shouted, "No, please, we have to go to the back yard and find my parents, my mother is buried alive." A policeman said, "We can't start digging, until we get some answers to some questions and the investigators get here." Ralph shouted, "Well, you will have to shoot me, because I am going to find my mother; she is in the flower garden."

Ralph ran outside to the garden, starting looking around, and then one of the policemen saw a pipe sticking out of the ground and said, "I see something sticking out of the ground over here." Ralph yelled, "That is where my mother is." One of the police officers asked, "How did you know where your mother was buried." Ralph yelled, "Because, that is where Rolf told me she was buried."

Ralph ran to the garden and began to dig. The police officers said, "Leave it alone until the investigators come." He started screaming, "Don't you understand, it is my mother, she may still be alive" as he kept digging. Some of the officers came over and helped him dig her up.

Then they felt her body, so they quickly jumped into the grave and pulled her out, with her still tied to the chair. Then they saw Mr. Chamberlain, underneath her, so they pulled him out, too. One of the officers felt for a pulse and shouted, "She is still alive." One of the other police officers, called for an ambulance.

Another one looked at Ralph and said, "Your mother will be alright but I am sorry your father is dead." Ralph collapsed to the ground, completely exhausted and filled with grief. Then the officers helped him up and Ralph went with his mother in the ambulance, to the hospital. After they arrived at the hospital Ralph, remembered that Rolf had told him that he had raped Rachel.

Before anyone could talk to Rachel the story was being told on the national television news. Back at the police station, Rolf was talking to anyone that would listen. The Chief of police asks him, "Ok Rolf what is it, that you want to tell me" as he looked at him. Rolf said, "I think someone needs to look at Rachel, because she has to be traumatized, by the brutal rape."

The Chief looked puzzled and called one of the arresting officers into his office. The Chief asks, "Did you find a woman that had been raped, in the house?" The officer stated, "No this is the first time, I heard about a rape victim. Rolf shouted, "I am telling you she needs help" The Chief said, "Where is she, so we can help her?" Rolf told him.

The Chief, called the police department in Okalahoma and they went to Mrs. Royal's, home to check on Rachel. When the police came into their home, he asked, "Do you know a man, by the name of Rolf Chamberlain?" Rachel began to tremble, as she said, "I know Ralph Chamberlain not Rolf."

The police officer said, "It is all over the news that a man, by the name of Rolf Chamberlain, Ralph Chamberlain's identical twin brother, has been arrested for killing his father Ralph Sr. and attempted murder of his mother, Victoria and brother Ralph and now Rolf Chamberlain said he traumatized you, by brutally raping you. Is that true?"

Rachel's mother began crying as she, screamed, "Yes, it is true, you have to help us" as she looked at Rachel. Rachel started crying, "Please, tell me, is Ralph alright?" the officer said, "Yes, I think he is, but he is at the hospital with his mother as we speak but you need help now." They took Rachel to the rape victim's unit at the hospital for help.

Back at the jail in Georgia, where Rolf was still talking about everything that he had done, a lawyer walked in and said, "Rolf stop talking and listen to me, I am your lawyer and I want to help you" so Rolf stopped talking. Rolf told his lawyer everything that he had done. However, he said to his lawyer, "I married Rachel and I want to keep her as my wife, she is mine now."

Back at the hospital Ralph asks one of the policemen, "Did you find out if Rachel is alright." He looked seriously at Ralph, "Yes and she had been raped, as your brother had said; "Now she is at the hospital in the rape victim's unit, in Okalahoma." Ralph began to cry, as the doctor came in and gave him a sedative, so he could sleep for the night.

The next morning the police inspectors were waiting to ask Ralph some questions. One of them approached him asking, "Mr. Chamberlain do you have any idea why, your brother may have behaved in such a manner?" Another officer asked, "Where did all his rage stem from?" Ralph said, "Well I will have to start from the beginning" so he did.

Ralph told Rolf's story, from childhood, until now and before he knew it, it was all over the news. The news media was asking, "How could something like this happen, a child hidden away all those year's." The people then understood Rolf's pain and anger, but shocked by his actions, too.

Rolf's lawyer knew all this information would help him with his case. Meanwhile, Ralph had to make arrangements for his father's funeral. Ralph walked into his mother's hospital room to speak to her. Teary eyed, he said, "Mother we have to make father's funeral arrangements" Victoria took Ralph's hand.

Victoria said, "I can't do this you will have too" he shook his head, "Yes" and walked into the lobby. Ralph looked up, saw Rachel and her mother standing there; they fell into each others arms and wept bitterly. Then Ralph looked into Rachel's eyes, saying, "I am so sorry for what my brother Rolf did to you."

Rachel looking up at him said, "I am sorry for what he did to all of us" as she reached down taking him, by the hand. Ralph said, "I have to make arrangements for my father's funeral, now." Rachel said, "Yes I know, I am here to help you." Mrs. Royal (Rachel's mother) said, "You two go ahead I will stay here with Victoria, she needs to know that we are here for her too."

So Ralph and Rachel left, to make the funeral arrangements. A few days later Victoria was out of the hospital, recovering from her ordeal and they were all sitting together at the funeral. The news media videotaped Victoria, Ralph, Mrs. Royal and Rachel all walking together, as they were leaving the funeral home.

Back at the jail, Rolf watched it all on the news with the other prisoners, but on one bothered him. They just left him alone. Strangely, Rolf felt sad for them, he knew what he had done was wrong, but at the same time, he felt justified. Ralph, Victoria, Mrs. Royal and Rachel stayed in a hotel awaiting Rolf's trial.

They simply could not go home where their ordeal had happened. Ralph hired contractors to go in and remodel the plantation home into what it should have been all along. In the meanwhile Ralph and Rachel rekindled their relationship and love for each other while awaiting the trial.

One day a police officer came to Rolf's cell laughing "Ha, Ha", "Well your wife Rachel is no longer YOUR wife!" Rolf shouted, "What do you mean she is mine and mine only!" Still laughing, "Ha, Ha" the officer said, "Not anymore, the judge just made your marriage contract invalid, null and void Ha, Ha." As he was walking away, he looked back saying, "Oh by the way your ex-wife, is pregnant with your child."

The officer continued, "I think she should get an abortion, to get rid of a crazy man's baby." Rolf's temper flared, he began to tear everything apart in his cell. The officers just stood there laughing at him. Rolf turned looking at them with his eyes glazed. "When I get out of here, I will kill you!" he shouted.

Ralph and Rachel married, however it was not the magnificent wedding they had hoped for, but they were together, that is all that mattered and Rolf could not stop them. Rachel was eight months pregnant when the trial started and everyone was seated in the courtroom waiting for the trail to begin.

However, when Rolf saw Rachel, he became furious and began to yell, "You are my wife, that is my baby and I will have him or her as mine one day" then he laughed, as a crazy man. The judge demanded that Rolf be taken from the courtroom immediately, Rachel held tightly to Ralph's arm.

As Rolf was being dragged from the courtroom, he yelled, "Wherever you go, or what ever you do, you will remember my words, I will be back!" Ralph looked at Rachel saying, "Don't worry I will protect you." But inside he felt helpless too. The trial took only three weeks. Everyone was sitting on the edge of their seats, awaiting the verdict to be read. The jury person stood up and read: "We the jury, have found Mr. Chamberlain guilty, of manslaughter, by the reason of insanity." Everyone was shocked, asking each other saying, "Why not 1st degree murder?"

However, it was a total shock when the judge read the sentence: "Mr. Chamberlain, you have been found guilty, by the jury of your peers and you are sentenced to the South Carolina institution, for the criminally insane for seven years." The courthouse was filled with outraged people asking, "How could this happen?"

Rolf overheard, Ralph screaming, "He killed my father, tried to kill my mother, raped my wife, how could this happen, seven years!" Rolf smiled at everyone as the officers hand-cuffed his hands behind his back and led him out of the courtroom, yelling, "Enjoy your life for awhile, because I will be back to finish the job."

Rolf was still in the local jail for a few more days, waiting to be transported to prison. One day an officer came by and said, "Mr. Chamberlain, you have a little girl, they named her Lara Victoria Chamberlain, they have victory over you." Rolf grabbed the officer by the throat; the other officers had to beat him off.

However, as for Ralph, Rachel and the rest of his family were finally happy, with their lives, at least for the next seven years........

CHAPTER 9

Rolf was in the Southeastern Institution for the criminally insane Now after seven long years, he had served his time. However, he had not gotten the help that he needed, but had become a master of deception. He had met other criminals that had taught him well, in a broad range of deceptions.

Reflecting back, all he wanted was revenge. Why should he be blamed for the murder of his father, attempted murder of his mother and raping his wife? After all in his mind, they drove him to do it. But, he had one good memory was of Ruby, his mother well the only mother he knew. He became angrier, as he thought about how his parents made her leave.

Nothing could console or comfort him, because anger had filled his life.

All he could think about was hurting someone, because he was hurting. As Rolf was standing at the desk in the institution getting his final papers from the officer; the officer said, "Now that you are released, I hope you have learned you lesson and will not get into anymore trouble.

Rolf said, "Yes I have learned my lesson well" while he was thinking, "Well enough not to get caught again." As he walked out of the doors, of the institution he looked around him seeing the trees, grass, and the sky all the things he could never see, as a child. And while he was in this place, he had been confined in a room with a small window, being able to see all these things, but still not able to touch them. He harbored all this in his heart.

He sat on a bench that was in the park, across the road from the institution, pondering all the things, in his mind and the anger came to a boiling point. He looked across the park and saw a lovely young woman sitting on another bench, reading a book. Rolf walked, over to her and said, "Hi would like to go for a cup of coffee."

Of course, she has no idea; he had just gotten out of the institution, she said, "Yes I would" after a few moments, of pause. She was beautiful, but naïve, as Rolf began leading her to the wooded part of the park, unawares to her, because she had her mind on talking. When they got to the edge of the woods, Rolf began looking around making sure no one else was in the park.

Looking at him with confusion, She asks, "What are you doing?" leaning down, He whispered in her ear, "I am going to rape you." The young lady began to cry, as she said, "Please my name is Dina Sharpe, my family has money, I can give you what ever you want, but please don't rape me, I am a virgin."

Rolf shouted, with anger in his voice, "That is even better" as he reached out to grab her. However, she began to run, but Rolf was taller and stronger. He pushed her to the ground, then picked her up and carried her back to the woods, with her kicking and screaming. She was terrified, tears flowing down her cheeks, as she begged, "Please don't do this, please."

Rolf climbed on top of her and felt her heart pounding, against his chest from the fear. He remembered all to well, his heart doing the same when Ruby, his only mother, had to leave him. But he still raped her, all the while, knowing and feeling, her fear. When he got up, she was afraid to move, as she was still looking at him with fear and confusion.

Rolf said, "I am leaving now, but you stay here for two hours," giving her his watch, so she would know when that would be. Then he gently, covered her up with her coat, while she was looking up at him with confusion in her eyes. Looking down at her with a serious look on his face, He whispered his last words, "If you tell anyone or if you scream and I have to come back, I will kill you" as he walked away.

Rolf thought he would feel better after hurting someone else, because of all his hurting he had going on inside himself. But all he felt was emptiness and not knowing how to solve his problem. He decided to go back home and finish killing, the rest of his family. But he was still a long way from home so he walked out to the edge of the road and held out his hand to hitchhike.

Soon a young man, stopped and asked, "Where are you going?" Leaning down to the car window, Rolf said, "Georgia" "Well I am not going that far, but you are welcome, to go as far as I can take you" he said. So Rolf got in the car, looking at the young man, with long brown hair pulled back into a ponytail, Slender with a tattoo on his left arm, of an angel.

Rolf asks, "Why an angel" pointing at the man's arm. As they were traveling slowly down the South Carolina, hills, the man said, "Well, I will tell you the story of my angel, but first let me tell you my name. It is Alen, now what is your name?" He said, "Rolf." Alen said, "Ok Rolf, I am going to tell you an amazing story.

He began, "When I was only eight years old, my family was in a horrific car wreck." "My mother and five year old sister were killed and I was left blind. My heart-broken father finished raising me alone." He continued, "But my father and I prayed, daily for my sight to return. Nevertheless I had to wait until I was twenty years old before, God answered that prayer."

Rolf asks, "How did it happen" Alen said, "Well, there was an old preacher, in our family that died and left a will, requesting his eyes to be donated to me. God answered that prayer in his time, not mine, but it was a miracle all the same." Rolf became angry, saying, "Let me out, I don't want to hear anymore of your story." But Rolf couldn't understand why he was angry; He just was.

As Alen drove off, he shouted, "Have a blessed day." Rolf turned his back to the man. Rolf began looking around, seeing how beautiful everything was, the land and the sky. After walking slowly in the snow for about an hour, Rolf was finally picked up, by another driver. This time it was an old man.

When Rolf approached the car, he looked at the old man, wrinkles on his face, silver hair and his lips were smiling. He said, "Hi, get in; my name is Henry, what is yours?" Rolf said, "I don't feel like talking, I just want a ride." Henry said, "I have no problem with that son." After a few minutes, Rolf looks around the car and sees the old man's key chain that read: There is no problem greater that God is.

Rolf angrily shouted, "Stop the car and let me out" the car came to a sudden stop, because the old man was shocked, by the shouting. Rolf got out and the old man, shaking a bit, drove off without a word spoken between them. For some reason Rolf felt bad, that the old man had gotten freighted of him, but shortly put it out of his mind.

He began walking again. However, after a few minutes he noticed a large yellow lab dog following him. Rolf began watching him wagging his tail back and forth and looking up at him, as if he knew him. But he wanted the dog to go away, for fear of having feeling for anything or anyone, so he started throwing rocks at the dog.

However, Rolf suddenly became ill and fell to the ground, he was trying to get up, but he just couldn't. The dog came and began licking Rolf, in the face, then turned and started darting in and out of the on coming traffic and back to Rolf again over and over; the car horns were blowing at the dog to get him out of the road, but they did not see Rolf lying there.

Rolf realized, the dog was trying to help, he was thinking, "Why would this dog want to help me, after being hit by the rocks, I was throwing at him." Finally, a police officer with lights flashing pulled on the side of the road to stop the dog, from getting hurt and saw Rolf lying there. The officer approached him, leaned down and told Rolf, "Sir I have called for help, we will have you in a hospital shortly."

Later, at the hospital the doctor, came in and told Rolf, "Sir you must have traveled a long way, because you are suffering from complete exhaustion." He continued, "Just rest here tonight and you can go home, in the morning." Rolf asks, "What happened to the dog that helped me?"

The doctor said, "I don't know about any dog, but I am sure if you ask, Officer Charles that brought you in; he will be glad to tell you in the morning, down at the police station." The doctor smiled as he turned and walked out of the room. The next morning….. Rolf went to the Police station to inquire about the dog.

He, nervously walked into the police station and asked, "Could I speak to Officer Charles?" The Officer behind the desk called, for Charles and when he saw Rolf, he said smiling, "You certainly look better than the last time, I saw you." Rolf showing no expression, said, "I would like to find out what happened to the dog that helped me."

Officer Charles replied, "We called his owner. The number was on his collar and he picked him up, but he left a three hundred dollar reward for you, let me get it for you." After he left the police station, disappointed and sad, Rolf went back to the road. After careful thought about what to do next, he decided to stay in South Carolina for awhile.

He went to the library, made his fake ID's he needed for his plastic surgeon degree, typed him an outstanding resume, bought a new suit with the three hundred dollars he got for the reward and walked into the administration office of the hospital and got a job. The only thing was the name on the fake ID's where, Ralph Chamberlain II.

No wonder it was easy for him to get a job, they could call anywhere except the job, Ralph II was really working and get excellent references. Rolf began working only three days later, at Frankford hospital in Frankford, South Carolina. Rolf was working with some, of the most renowned plastic surgeons in the world and loving every minute of it.

After a year, Rolf volunteered to take care of the poor inside their homes, if it where small procedure's, because they didn't have the money for it, to be done in the hospital. However, no one was unaware that he was raping the women patients once they were under the anesthesia.

He had been raping and performing surgery on the poor, all his second year in Frankford.

He knew that these people would not tell, because they were getting their services free and wasn't sure, as to what happened to them. And the people, having no proof, silence were the best choice, after all who would believe them anyway, that was Rolf's thoughts on the matter. Later at the hospital, while Rolf was walking down the hall, he noticed a former face coming toward him.

The administrator, Mr. Howl smiled as he shouted, "Ralph you will never guess who stopped in for a visit, an old friend of yours" of course he was speaking to Rolf unaware. The former face was Dr. Edward Kennedy, from Paris that had taught Ralph, Rolf recognized him from the pictures his brother had sent home with his letters, telling about him.

Rolf trying to think quickly, before they got any closer "What can I say to a man I have never met" Dr. Kennedy stretched out his hand "It is very nice to see you again, Ralph." "Like-wise" smiling trying not to give him away. Dr. Kennedy said, "Ralph you seem different somehow, but that is what time does to us all I suppose."

"Yes I suppose so, could you two excuse me, I am expected in surgery soon" shaking inside as he walked away, looking at his watch, so not to be recognized. The administrator, Mr. Howl smiled, "That man works entirely too much" "Well he hasn't changed much then" stated, Dr. Kennedy as they went on their way.

Rolf stayed hid the rest of Dr. Kennedy's visit, as he pretended to have entirely too much work to do to visit at all; and his volunteer work helped with his excuse. Later Mr. Howl asks, "Ralph, why didn't you want to visit with your friend while he was here, I thought you two were close."

Of course Rolf did not want to talk about it, all he wanted to do was walk away, but he had to give some type of an answer "Well we were, but as colleagues, not friends." "Oh I see" they walked away, not saying another word about it. Later that day Rolf had scheduled minor surgery, in the home of a young widow woman of three years, Isabelle Altman.

Rolf felt that if he could hurt her, by raping her he would feel better, about the tension he had to endure from Dr. Kennedy's visit. So that is what he set out to do. When he got to her small quiet country home, he first set everything up for the surgery. Then he put her to sleep, with the anesthesia, while he was looking at her sleeping; she was so beautiful long black hair, softly lying across the pillow.

Her soft skin, with the perfect face and body, her only fault was the mole Rolf was there to remove, from her shoulder. Rolf was ready to do the surgery and thinking, "After this procedure, I will still have time to rape her, before she wakes up." He put on his gloves and as he turned around to begin. Out of corner of his eye he noticed something move behind the door of the room.

He stopped and looked, as a little girl came out from behind the door. The little girl walked over to him, looking up into his eyes and said, "I see through your eyes, into your empty soul, with no hope, no filling of the spirit of God." Shocked, by her words thinking, "What wisdom coming from this little girl" Rolf stepped back; as she continued, "God can do all things, he can give to your soul love, hope, forgiveness and wipe away all the hurts and sorrows from your heart, because he loves you."

Rolf was so emotionally overwhelmed; he dropped to his knees, knowing the truth for the first time that he was not going to be fulfilled, the way he was going. The only way was with God's help. Now he realized God loved him and he was there all the time. He cried bitter tears, as he released all the pain and bitterness from his heart, asking, "God help me, please?"

He knew that, God had reached into his soul and forgiven him and made him a new person within his soul. The little girl hugged him saying, "Now you can be happy" and he was thinking, "If this little girl, had not been here at this moment, I would not be saved and the woman would be hurt."

Rolf smiled, as he asked, "What is your name little girl?" She replied, "My name is Darlene, I am five years old and that is my mommy lying there" He said, "Yes and you have a beautiful mommy, now I need you to leave this room so I can do surgery on her." She started skipping away, singing Jesus loves me, this I know.

By the time Rolf got back to the hospital, Dr. Edward Kennedy had gone home, he was thinking, "What a relief that was and the administrator was none the wiser." Over the next few weeks Rolf stopped by weekly to check on Isabelle. Isabelle invited him to church and soon they were going to church regularly and studying the Bible together.

Rolf learned what falling in love with a woman was really all about true love. He had learned what family life was supposed to be like, and he loved being a Christian. It brought a whole new prospective to light. After dating for six months Rolf said, "Isabelle I have fallen in love with you and Darlene, please marry me?"

Before she had a chance to answer, Rolf looking at her, smiling said, "I feel so blessed that God touched me and saved me." "I know now, that God had been working on me for awhile, but I did not realize it, until I met your daughter." Isabelle looked up at him and said, "My answer is, yes" they embraced.

One day, they were talking about the wedding plans and Isabelle said, "Honey, we have to call your family, you know they would like to come to your wedding." He looked seriously at her and said, "I will have to tell you all about my family, someday, but until that time comes, please just trust me, I can't invite them to our wedding."

She looked at him with total trust, saying, "Yes I trust you with all of my heart" and said no more about his family. Rolf said, "I am happier than I have ever been in my life." He added, "What do you think about us buying a home, before we get married?" Darlene heard him and started shouting, "Yes, yes let's buy a new house with a big back yard to play in, ok."

Isabelle said, "What ever you say dear," and they all hugged. Later, they found the home that they all agreed on, a large three bedroom, two and a half bath, on one acre lot. They got married in their backyard on June twelfth. It was a small beautiful wedding. A few days later, Rolf had play ground equipment brought into the back yard, as a surprise for Darlene.

When Darlene saw it, she said, "Thank you daddy" and hugged him. Rolf was shocked, that she called him daddy, but was very happy at the same time. He said, "You know that you and your mother are the light of my life and I love you, both" and hugged her and kissed her, on the top of the head.

One day three months later, Rolf was sitting in the back yard thinking, about all the hurt he had done to everyone, his brother, dad, mother, sister-in-law and the other women. He began to cry, holding his face with his hands, he was crying so hard that he did not realize Isabelle was approaching him.

When she heard him crying, she ran to him, asking, "Honey, what it, what is wrong?" as she wrapped her arms around him. He held her tight saying, "I wish I could tell you, but now is not the time." She said, "You can tell me anything, at anytime, don't you know that." But he did not tell her that day.

As time went on he realized, that he had the calling of God on his life, to become a preacher. He told Isabelle, about the call of God on his life and she and Darlene were both excited. But, he said to Isabelle, "I have you talk to you alone first" so they walked outside to sit on the bench, in the backyard.

Rolf took her the hand, and said, "Isabelle I have to reveal my past, to you and my true identity." She looked at him with shock and confusion, "What do you mean, your true identity, you are Ralph Chamberlain my husband and surgeon at the hospital." He looked at her with tears of sadness, "No I am Rolf Chamberlain, Ralph Chamberlain is my brother and we are both surgeons."

Still in shock, with tears streaming down her cheeks, she said, "No you are Ralph Chamberlain, why are you saying that you are not, I don't understand." He said, "Please don't cry, I changed my name when I came to this town, to start over and I wanted to forget my past." "But then I met you and Darlene and my life truly started over; but, before I can go on with God and preach I have to set the record straight."

Isabelle said, "Of course you can tell me anything." After taking a deep breath, He began, "when I was a child I was locked away, from the rest of my family because I had a deformed face, but my brother helped me get my education online, while he got his in Paris and we, became plastic surgeons and he repaired my face."

He continued, "After the surgery, something else happen and I felt that Ralph had betrayed me, as everyone else had in my life, so I snapped and hurt him, my father, mother and anyone else that got in my way. There was a trail and I was sent to an institution for the criminally insane, where I stayed for seven long years."

She began to shake, saying, "How could I not know, that you were like that and I let you around my child" he tried to hug her, but she walked away and ran into the house. He shouted, "Isabelle I am not that person anymore, God saved me and forgave me. The person I am telling you about is not standing in front of you now." But he let her go, so she could ponder his words and come to her own decision. He knew he could not force the issue.

Isabelle ran into the bedroom, fell across the bed and cried for hours. Darlene came into her mother's bedroom and said, "Mommy I heard what my step daddy said. He is right, he is not the man you first met, he is filled with God's goodness now, so please forgive him and love him, you married the saved one, not the one he told you about.

Isabelle looked at her and said, "My little precious Darlene, you have the wisdom of God on your side. You are right and I do love and forgive him; if God forgave him, then who am I? So Isabelle walked back in the living room, where Rolf was and wrapped her arms around his neck, as she turned looking into his eyes saying, "You are right, I did not know that person, you were talking about."

Isabelle continued, "But I do know you, God forgave and so do I.

I love you with all of my heart" Rolf let out a sigh of relief and they embraced.

Rolf said, a silent prayer, "Thank you, **God**" and said, "Isabelle you and Darlene are my life, God has been good to me, even though I do not deserve it.

Isabelle said, "God does not forgive us, because we deserve it, or work for it, but because our heart has changed toward Him. Darlene said, "I am so happy that God gave me this family. Are you two happy with our family?" Looking up at them Rolf smiled, "Yes, we are little one" as he picked her up into his arms and gave her hug.

He legally changed his name as it should be, as Rolf Chamberlain. Then, he was anointed to preach, went to a preacher's conference as Rolf Chamberlain, not Ralph and later he was given a church in the state of Pennsylvania. Their family was happy and living a great life. Rolf was in full time ministry and Isabelle was a full time homemaker.

One day, about six months into his preaching, Isabelle came to Rolf, as he was sitting in the swing in the backyard. He looked up at her and asked, "What is that big smile on your face all about?" She placed her hand on his shoulder and said, "Well honey, we are going to have a baby." He leaned back in the swing, for a moment of shock.

Darlene had walked outside and overheard the news. She started jumping up and down with excitement shouting, "I am going to have a little brother or sister, Hooray!" Isabelle looked, at Rolf asking; "Are you happy about our news?" he jumped up, hugging her saying, "Darling I could not be happier than I am right now."

Rolf starting thinking, about his own childhood and wondering how anyone could neglect or hurt their child, as his parents did; but then he knew the things he had done and knew that it takes God to help a person do the right thing and knew in his heart at that moment that he needed to pray for his family to be saved, so he did.

Shortly after he began to preach, he was approached to have his sermons televised and he agreed, hoping that he could reach his family also. Rolf was soon becoming famous; because, God had blessed him with a great speaking ability. Soon it was time for Isabelle to give birth to the baby.

However, when they arrived at the hospital Isabelle asks, "Rolf please stay out here with Darlene I will alright" as she hugged him. He said, "But my place is with you" she looked at him, with tears swelling up in her eyes and again said, "Please Rolf, stay out here with Darlene" so he did.

While he was waiting, in the waiting room he began to think, "I wonder if something is wrong, with her or the baby? Is that why she did not want me in the delivery room with her?" He was feeling helpless, not being able to help Isabelle. Darlene put her little arms around his neck and said, "Daddy we can pray" so they did.

After about four hours of passing back and forth and Darlene following right behind him, his nerves where on edge. Finally, a nurse came out holding a little baby. The nurse look at Rolf, smiling as she said, Mr. Chamberlain, you have a baby boy. Rolf quickly uncovered his baby, checking him out from head to toe.

Then he looked at the nurse, smiling from ear to ear and said, "He is perfect." He began to cry as he looked at his perfect, no flawed little baby. The nurse began to laugh; "Of course he is what did you expect?" She did not understand where Rolf was coming from. Darlene was watching Rolf too. She was so excited as she said to Rolf, "Daddy, I have a perfect little brother. Just look at him."

The nurse took him to the nursery. But a short time later, the same nurse was coming back down the hall, with the baby again. Rolf's heart began racing, as he asks, "What is wrong, why are you bringing him back?" The nurse said, "Please don't worry, nothing is wrong, as she kept walking toward him, until she reached the waiting room.

She said, "Mr. Chamberlain, this is your other son" Rolf had to sit down as he asks, "Excuse me, but did you say other son, we have two boys?" The nurse said, "Yes you do." Rolf's heart sank, "Oh no, what if this one was born like me?" he quickly uncovered him, checking him head to toe and he was identical to his brother, perfect, with no flaws. He started crying again.

The nurse began to laugh again, as she watched this new father checking out his new born son. But, when Rolf realized, he had two perfectly formed babies he cried, "Oh thank you, God for all your blessings on me." Of course, the nurse did not have a cue, as to what all this was all about. The nurse, turned to take the baby back to the nursery, but Rolf asks, "Wait, can I see my wife now?" She looked back at him and said, "Of course, follow me."

When Rolf walked into Isabelle's room, smiling and looking at her, he said, "Honey, you never looked as beautiful as you do right now" he kissed her. Then he said, "We have twins" she replied, "Yes I know" He asks, "How long have you known that we were going to have twins?"

Smiling at him, she said, "Only a couple of weeks, but I just wanted to surprise you, did you ever think that we could have two, isn't it wonderful" Rolf stated, "Yes" and kissed her again. Isabelle said, "Well you know we have to choose a name for our boys, what shall it be?" Rolf replied, "Well we have already chosen Wesley, if it was a boy, so what do you think of Lesley?" She said, "Prefect Wesley and Lesley it is."

Darlene was standing in the hallway waiting for her turn to come in, when she shouted, "I am in the hallway waiting, can I come in now?" Isabelle and Rolf looked at each other laughing, "Ha, Ha, Ha" as Rolf went to the door, and let her in. Before, Rolf began to preach on Sunday morning, Rolf was proud to announce to the people of the church, that there were two additions to their church family now.

Rolf said, "Next Sunday, we will have two new members "Wesley and Lesley, my new sons that were born January 8th" and the people clapped their hands and smiled. Then they heard a small voice shout, "And my new brothers" coming from the front pew and they laughed, as they looked at Darlene.

Life was wonderful, they brought their boys home from the hospital and everything was great. Darlene wanted to help with her little brothers and she wasn't jealous, much. One day Rolf was in a meeting with several other pastors. He was holding Lesley in his arms and in the middle of the meeting; Lesley threw up all over his shirt. He excused himself and went upstairs to change.

However, after him changing his clothes, he saw that Wesley needed a diaper change; just as he took off his diaper, Wesley wet all over the front of his shirt and he had to change again. When Rolf got back down stairs, he told the other pastors and they all laughed, as they where telling him, they understood, because they had children too.

When the boys were six months, they began to crawl, Wesley was always first and Lesley would copy him. It was funny watching them, because they started out trying to crawl backwards. Rolf and Isabelle videotaped it all. Wesley and Lesley were happy babies and giggled about everything.

Once at church, the boys were sitting on the floor and they began to race each other crawling and giggling at the same time. Rolf was trying to preach to the congregation, but, had to stop for Isabelle to pick them up they from the floor, while the people were laughing, everyone always thought Wesley and Lesley were so cute, what ever they were doing.

Later when the boys where eighteen months old, the family was sitting at the dining room table eating spaghetti, when Wesley picked up his plate and turned it over, sitting it on top of his head, all the while smiling. By this time the family had a camera close by, so they could take pictures of all the crazy things they did.

Darlene snapped the picture, while Isabelle grabbed a towel to clean everything up, when Lesley picked up his plate and did the same thing and everyone laughed and Wesley and Lesley giggled too.

Rolf was preaching and had become famous, throughout the United States and his preaching was now, reaching around the world. The boys were growing, now they were three years old and Isabelle said to Rolf, "Rolf please stop preaching for awhile, we have to have a break." Rolf said, "Honey I can't stop preaching, but we can take a vacation, how would you like that?"

Isabelle replied, "That would be wonderful" so they planned for a vacation.............

CHAPTER 10

The entire country had become aware of Rolf's great presence in the religious culture, for his evangelism. However, His preaching tour had begun to take its toll on his family life. As a result he decided to take a much needed two-week vacation, with his family. Finally, they were on their way to Six Flags, in Atlanta Georgia and leaving the state of Wisconsin, where Rolf had finished his preaching tour, at the present.

Now that everything was packed and Isabelle saw that everyone was in the car and they, were moving down the road Isabelle finally began to relax saying to Rolf, "I am so blessed, to be able to call you, my husband," as she laid her hand, on Rolf's shoulder. He turned his head, looking at her smiling, "I hate to correct you, my dear, but I am the one that is blessed, to have someone as wonderful as you to come into my life."

Rolf peered behind his seat, to see his daughter sleeping silently, her head leaning, against the window "We have an amazing daughter, to be able to speak words of wisdom, to win someone like me, to God." "Yes, I know God, has given her a way with words, that amazes so many and I am so proud of her," said Isabelle.

They began, joyfully singing: Amazing grace, how sweet the sound, that saved a wretch like me…. and talking, about their family's future plans. Rolf stated, "You know, Wisconsin is a beautiful state, although I would not want to live here, because of the cool weather, it is a beautiful place to visit," as he was looking out the window, at the country, as they passed by.

Isabelle smiling, "Yes, it is beautiful here, the air is fresh and the lakes are so clear." He looked at her, as to say, "Yes let's come back so I can fish," smiling, he replied, "Yes, a great place for FISHING, and the tall trees, especially the blue-purrs tree, make for great scenery." "The people seem content and at peace. Especially the dairy farmers seem to love it here." She said.

And she added, "Yes, we can come back, so we ALL can go fishing" as they began to laugh, "Ha, Ha." Isabelle said, "Look we are in the state of Illinois" as she was pointing to the sign, that read, Welcome to the sate of Illinois. The children jumped up, to see, but they were not impressed and fell back in their seats.

They had been traveling for several hours and Wesley and Lesley were becoming restless, turning upside down in the seat, their head hanging down to the floor, falling to the floor crying, as three year-old children will do and Darlene shouting, "they are hurting me" as a nine year-old child will do and everyone was ready to stop for the night.

Rolf jokingly said, "Ok everyone, I need your help, to find a hotel" Wesley jumped up and shouted, "I will help you daddy" "No me," shouted Lesley, as he pushed his brother out of his way. Isabelle turns, to look at them and shouted, "Now boys, Daddy needs everyone's help," as she smiled at them and they smiled back, at her.

Darlene said, "Daddy I am hungry for some french-fries" Wesley said, "Me too" Lesley shouted, "No me tooo...." As they were coming off, interstate 89 they began entering into a small quiet town, except for the children making their noise, of course. Isabelle said, "Honey, I think we might have to stop for a bite to eat, before going to the hotel."

However, shortly after the turn off, Rolf became uneasy, as he notices a car fast approaching them, weaving back and forward, behind them. He was trying to listen to Isabelle and watching this crazy driver behind him, at the same time. He shouted, "Isabelle watch out for the children, there is a crazy driver behind us."

Suddenly, there was a loud crash, as the two cars collide into each other. Everyone was screaming and holding on to each other, as the cars hooked together. And the cars were sliding down the road, finally coming to a sudden stop about one hundred yards; as the side of their car slammed into a tree, stopping both cars.

Shocked, bewildered and trying to think about what had just happen, they heard a woman yelling, "I am a nurse, just be still, I can help" as she approached their car on the passenger side and looked at Isabelle. "I am Nancy Greene, a nurse at Centerville hospital, just down the road, I have already called 911 and given them the location of your accident" all the while, she was visually examining each one, in the car.

Isabelle slowly and painfully, (because she was hurting) turned to look in the back seat to find that all of her screaming children were injured. Nancy said, "Try not to move until the ambulance gets here, we do not know how serious anyone is hurt" as she opened the back door, to examine the screaming children.

Rolf got out of the car praying loudly, "Please Oh God let everyone be alright, protect them, please." However, he could not get to the back door on his side to examine the children, because it was jammed against the tree, shocked, as he saw Darlene was bleeding from the head and not moving he knew it was serious.

He grabbed the first aid kit from under the front seat and he had to wrap Darlene' head, by leaning over the front seat to reach to the back and trying not to move her anymore than necessary. Nancy looked at the silent little girl (Darlene) and then looked at the man (Rolf)'s face, as it was filled with fear for his child, she knew it was bad, but Rolf was taking care of her, so the she began caring for the boys (Wesley and Lesley).

Wesley yelled, "Mommy, I have a bad boo boo, it hurts, put a ban aide on it pleaseee!" Wesley shouted, "Hold me, mommy" as his arms were reaching out to her. Isabelle got out of the car to help her children, but Nancy said, "You can't move them until the ambulance gets here; you may hurt them worse, by moving them."

Isabelle did not know what to do, so she stood back to watch, as she said comforting words to them, "It will be alright, just listen to this nice lady, Ms. Nancy and your father, but try not to move, ok." Lesley screamed, "Mommy, Mommy I want you hold me, mommy......" Isabelle still repeating, her words of comfort to the boys, "It will be alright just listen to Ms. Nancy, she is a nurse alright" while tears were flowing down her face.

Nancy saw that Wesley obviously had his right leg broken, so she gently supported his broken leg and laid him in the front seat, while he was screaming of course. Isabelle shouted, "Why did you move him, I thought moving them, may hurt them worse?" Nancy said, "I need to see what is going on with your other son, so can you comfort the one in the front seat, please."

Isabelle crying, "God please help us; don't let my children be in pain, Oh God please."However, Nancy asked, Lesley "What is your name and where do you hurt?" He said, with his lips quivering, "My name is Lesley, my legs wouldn't move" as he was screaming and tears flowing down his face, "Mommy, Mommy."

Isabelle sat down, in the back seat and held Lesley's hand. She also reached to the front seat and held Wesley's hand too, saying, "I love you my babies."As tears were flowing down her cheeks, she looked at Rolf caring for Darlene, asking, "How is she?" he looked at her, saying with his voice trembling, "Everything will be alright," but he was not sure, because it was a head injury.

Finally, two ambulances arrived and Nancy shouted, "You will have to take the little boy in the front seat first, he has a broken leg, so be careful" as the EMT took him and placed him on the stretcher. By this time, a group of people had formed in the street and the police had to make them back up.

One person, said to another, "I think that is that evangelist Rolf Chamberlain from TV," someone else said, "Yes, I think you are right," so they began calling other people, they knew, to tell them and soon it was on the news. Two other EMT's came walking toward the car, with a stretcher when, Nancy said, "This little boy is paralyzed from the waist down, so be careful with his back" they put a neck brace on, as they were laying him down on the stretcher.

Isabelle heard what was said and starting crying, "Oh my God, he is paralyzed." Rolf ran around the car, reached in the back seat and carefully removed Darlene and gently placed her on one of the stretchers,' saying, "Take her first, because of her head injury" meaning, before checking himself out.

Now the two boys were taken to one ambulance, by the EMT's on their stretchers, Wesley screaming with his broke leg and Lesley with an unknown problem, because his legs had no feeling. Both the boys were screaming, "Mommy, Daddy help me don't leave me." One of the EMT's said, "Mr. and Mrs. Chamberlain, you two need to be checked too."

Rolf said, "We will have to wait the children are the ones that seem to be hurt the worse, so concentrate on them, for now." Isabelle looked up at Rolf and asks, "Rolf, please tell me our children are going to be alright and why isn't Darlene making any sound." Rolf said, "Everything is going to be ok. Let's just get to the hospital for now, you ride with the boys and I'll ride with Darlene."

Then, they over heard some of the people in the crowd, saying, "You know the man that hit them was drunk and that little girl will probably die, don't you see her bleeding from the head." Isabelle quickly looked up at Rolf again and he said, "Don't listen to them, she will all be alright."

Nevertheless, on the way to the hospital Isabelle was hysterical and Rolf was trying to keep his emotions together for his family. When he got into the ambulance, away from Isabelle and the boys he broke down and cried. The EMT asked, "Mr. Chamberlain would you like to lie down too" "No, I have to be here for my daughter" he replied, as tears were flowing.

Rolf looked at Darlene laying there so small and helpless, as he began to pray, "God please let my child live, I just don't know if I can take it, if I lose her, after all I would not be where I am with you, if it where not for her, please help us all." Finally, they arrived at the hospital still in shock. The police were there to meet them for questioning, as just what had happened in the accident.

The nurse, Nancy came up to the policeman and said, "I saw the whole thing, let me tell you so this family can be checked out for injuries" as she waived to Rolf and Isabelle to go with their children. So the policeman replied, "We can get your report now and their report later" and so after getting the police report out of the way for now, they went with the children, Rolf looked back at Nancy saying, "Thank-you."

Rolf and Isabelle saw that the hospital was small, but efficient; three doctors were on call that night and a neurosurgeon was called in for Darlene. Rolf was not thinking straight, as he spoke to the surgeon and explained, "I am a doctor also and I want to assist in the surgery" as he was looking at the surgeon, with fear in his eyes for his child's welfare.

The surgeon said, "Now Mr. Chamberlain you know, I can't allow you to do that. You are too emotionally involved with the patient." Rolf shouted, with tears coming down his cheeks, "There is no way I am staying out of the operating room" The surgeon replied, "Very well however, you can not assist in the actual surgery" Rolf said, "Very well" as they where going toward the operating room with Darlene.

Darlene was still unconscious, as they went into the operating room for surgery. Rolf looked at Isabelle and hugged her, as he said, "Honey, I am going into the operating room with Darlene, please take care of the boys and say prayers for all of us." She said, "I will" as she had tears flowing down her cheeks, he kissed her on top of the head and walked away with the other doctor.

After Rolf left the room Isabelle fainted, from all the over whelming stress going on around her. When she came to, there was a nurse standing over her bed, she was the nurse Nancy that helped at the accident. Isabelle asks, "How are my children?" Nancy said, "Your boys are fine, Wesley has a cast on his leg and Lesley's paralysis is temporary, but you have a lot of bruising and you need to rest.

The nurse also added, "Darlene is still in surgery." Isabelle asks, "Do you think my daughter Darlene, will be ok?" Nancy said, "I am sure she will be" Isabelle gave a sigh of relief. Nancy said, "But, you have some people that are asking to see you. Do you want me to let them in?" Isabelle asks, "Who is it?" Nancy stated, "They are your in-laws."

Isabelle was puzzled, thinking "I wonder why they are here and how in the world did they know that we are here, as well especially since we have never met" as she said, "Really, well let them in" so Nancy opened the door and Victoria, Ralph, and Rachel walked in the room.

Shocked and confused, Isabelle looked at Ralph asking, "Rolf, what are you doing?" because she had never met them, so she thought she was seeing Rolf. Ralph smiled, saying "I am sorry that we have never met, I am Ralph, Rolf's identical twin brother" Isabelle holding her head, trying to take everything in at once, said, "I had no idea that you looked identical to Rolf."

Victoria sighed with relief, that Rolf was not in the room, as she said, "My dear, I am your mother-in-law and this is Rachel, your sister-in-law" as she pointed to Rachel. Isabelle still looking a bit confused, as she asks, "How did you know that we were here?" Ralph smiled saying, "It is on the news, that the TV evangelist Rolf Chamberlain and his family was in an auto accident and it just so happened, that we were vacationing near by."

Then he added, "When we heard about your tragedy and we felt that your family needed us to be here." Isabelle taking a deep breath replied, "You are so right, we needed our family to be with us now, thank-you for coming" they hugged her. The doctor came into Isabelle's room and said, "Mrs. Chamberlain we have to take some x-rays of you to see what is going on, if anything because you are badly bruised."

Victoria said, "I will go with you dear," as she took her by the arm to help her out of bed. Isabelle looked up at the doctor and asks, "What about my children?" The doctor said, "They are fine, but you need assistance now, follow me." Isabelle said, "Thank-you," turned to look at Ralph and Rachel asking, "Will you two look after my boys, while I am gone, they are in the children's wing room 202, and their names are Wesley and Lesley."

They looked surprised, because they did not know; Rolf had children but said, "Of course, we will." Ralph and Rachel walked down the hall to room 202 and saw the two little three year olds sleeping in their beds. Ralph said, "They are so small and look so sweet" but, Wesley began reaching out his little arms, crying "Mommy, Mommy" in his sleep. Rachel held his hand and he began to clam down and stopped crying.

She said, "Ralph my love, please go down to the gift shop and buy two teddy bears, I think if they had something to hold on to, they could sleep better" "Yes dear," as he walked out of the room. In a few minutes, he came back with two brown teddy bears and the boys held them, in their sleep.

They walked back down to Isabelle's room, to wait for her. However, down the hall Rolf and the doctor was coming out of Darlene's surgery. They overheard someone laughing, "I think, I was in an accident, but I am not sure, ha, ha, ha" and as they turned the corner, it was the drunk driver that had hit them. Rolf felt that old feeling of rage come over him and he said, "I'm going to kill you."

Two police officers where standing near by, when they saw Rolf's face, they ran and grabbed his arms, stopping him from attacking the man. Rolf was shouting, at the man, "How could you hurt my children like this." However the man was so drunk, he did not even know what he had done.

One of the officers told, Rolf, "Mr. Chamberlain, we are here to take this man to jail for what he did, to your family. Don't worry." Rolf shouted, "Don't worry, we could have all been killed and you say don't worry," as he was shaking his finger in the officer's face." The Officer understood, how Rolf felt, because he had a family too.

The doctor shouted, to the officers, "Please hold him for me" as he gave Rolf a sedative to calm him down for the night. Then the doctor asked, "Will you please, follow me" The officers carried him, into a room and laid Rolf down on the bed. The exhausted doctor walked down to Isabelle's room, to tell her all the news.

When he walked into the room, he introduced himself to everyone (Ralph, Victoria and Rachel) and asked, "Mrs. Chamberlain, may I speak to you alone." She took a deep breath to brace herself for anymore bad news that may come and said, "Please doctor, just tell me about my daughter."

Scratching his head, thinking he said, "Well, Mrs. Chamberlain, we will have to see what the next forty-eight hours brings." As he reached down, he took her by the hand to comfort her. Isabelle began to cry, "Where is my husband?" The doctor said, "I am sorry, but he was so upset I had to give him a sedative, so he could sleep for a while."

Shocked, as she looked at the doctor frantically Isabelle asked, "Oh no was he that upset about our daughter? Doesn't he think she will make it?" The doctor trying to calm her said, "No it is not that it is just that he saw the drunk driver that hit your car." She said, "The drunk driver is here in this hospital" he said, "He was but now he is in jail."

Tears heavily dropping from her eyes Rachel softly said, "We are here for you and we will be here as long as you need us" as she walked over and hugged Isabelle. Ralph walked down the hall to see the boys, but they were still asleep and over heard, the doctor calling the nurse in the room and said, "Give Mrs. Chamberlain a sedative so she can sleep for the night." When the nurse came into the room with the sedative, Victoria said, "We need to let everyone rest for the night and come back in the morning." The nurse said, "Yes, Mrs. Chamberlain needs a good night's sleep too and everyone can go the hotel and come back in the morning." So they all said their good-bye's as Isabelle was falling to sleep and left for the night.

When they got to the hotel they sat down at the table in Victoria's room to have a conversation. Rachel said, "I know that we have been watching Rolf on TV preaching to everyone, but I still remember what he did to me and it is really hard knowing we will be in the same room with him in the morning" as she tightly held on to Ralph's hand.

Victoria angrily looking at Ralph shouted, "Yes and he killed your father and tried to kill me are you forgetting that Ralph?" Ralph softly said, "No I am not forgetting any of the things he has done however, listening to him on the TV I got saved and I think you two need to face him so you can stop being afraid that he may come back to hurt you. You can see if he has truly changed or not."

He also added, "If you listen to Isabelle, she does not know the person that did those things and it is because he has truly changed into that person you see on TV. Victoria shouted, "I think the whole thing is ludicrous" Rachel looked at Ralph saying, "I trust you and I will do this because you think it will help with our healing somehow, but it is the last time I ever want to see him."

Victoria turned throwing her hand on her hip shouting, "Ok if Rachel is going then so will I but I am going to give him a piece of my mind" Ralph looked seriously at both of them saying, "Say what ever you like to him, just try not to hurt his family they had nothing to do with it. Now let's all say good-night" and they went to bed.

The next morning when Rolf woke up he saw his mother (Victoria), his brother (Ralph) and Rachel (Ralph's wife) standing at the end of his bed.

Ralph walked over and hugged Rolf, Victoria fearfully gave a half grin but stayed back and Rachel held on to Ralph's hand as she shook Rolf's hand then backed up.

Rolf began to sob as he was saying, "Thank-you for coming I know it was hard for you and I understand but thank-you all the same." Rolf got up quickly saying, "I am sorry but I have to go check on my children now would you like to come?" They followed him down to Isabelle's room.

When Rolf walked into her room Isabelle was getting out of bed and he walked over to her, took her gently by the hand, and together they began walking to Darlene's room. Victoria and Ralph were watching how gentle Rolf took Isabelle by the hand and how concerned he was for his children.

The boys were crying so loud they had to stop to see them first. The nurses had them in the same room, but they wanted their mommy and daddy. When Rolf and Isabelle walked in Wesley and Lesley wrapped their little arms around their necks holding tight and did not want to let go.

The doctor came in and said, "The boys are ok Lesley's feeling in his legs has completely come back and Wesley's leg is going to take a few weeks to heal and they can be released anytime you are ready to take them." While the doctor is telling Rolf, Isabelle, Victoria and Ralph about the children Rachel is visiting with Darlene.

When Rachel walks in the room with Darlene, Darlene looks at her and asks, "Who are you" "I am your aunt Rachel I am married to your uncle Ralph" replied Rachel. Darlene asks, "Have you met my mommy and daddy and brothers?" "Yes I have" said, Rachel. She asks, "Did you know my daddy is a preacher now?"

Rachel said, "Yes I heard but I only knew him when he was filled with anger and did bad things" "But now he is a kind, gentle person that loves everyone" replied, Darlene. Rachel could not stand it any longer so she shouted, "No one can change that much" Darlene smiled saying, "Yes they can if they accept **Jesus** in their heart, and he did."

Darlene continued, "If **God** can forgive then why can't you?" as she reached out and took Rachel's hand and she began to cry Darlene said, "It is alright." Back in the boys room Rolf asks, "What about Darlene how is she," looking at the doctor's face for the hope he desperately needed.

The doctor sadly said, "She is awake but I am very sorry to tell you it is just a matter of time" Rolf ran to her room however, when they walked into her room Rachel was standing by her bed. Darlene was telling Rachel about Rolf's first experience with God how on his knees he cried bitter tears and was saved.

Rachel turned to look at Rolf with tears coming down her cheeks now believing in an all powerful God with his love can change the heart of a murderer and rapist into a true child of God. Rolf smiled as he looked at the miracle of forgiveness as Rachel forgave him and was instantly healed from all the hurting in her heart as God forgave her of her sins too, whatever they made have been.

Rolf walked over to the bed and gently hugged Darlene for fear of hurting her. He said, "I love you little one" she said, "I love you too daddy, how is Wesley and Lesley" as she looked at her mommy. Isabelle said, "They are fine your uncle and grandmother are holding them out in the hall." She leaned down to hug Darlene too.

The doctor came in and said. "Can I speak with you two in the hall" as he looked at Rolf and Isabelle. When they walked out into the hall he said, "Did you two understand when I said it is only a matter of time for Darlene?" Suddenly reality hit them as they realized what the doctor was saying Darlene is going to die, Rolf looked at Isabelle with tears in his eyes and said, "I can not believe God is going to take her away from us."

Isabelle fainted again. When she came to she began cry hysterically Rolf held her ever so gently. That is when Victoria and Ralph realized that he really had changed and how much he loved his family. Ralph said, "Rolf we can take the boys home with us so you and Isabelle can stay here with Darlene"

The doctor said, "That is a good idea but you two decide." With a whimper Rolf asks them, "Could you please take them home with you today?" "Of course we will." All were in agreement. "Before you leave with them please let them say good-bye to their sister" Isabelle grasped for the words, her eyes swollen, soon tears starting to roll down her rosy cheeks again.

The two boys reaching for Isabelle were slowly lifted from their bed.

The grief was taking its toll on them. Their bodies felt heavy from the load Isabelle and Rolf slowly walked them down the hallway to say good-bye to the sister they loved so much. As they entered her room and were close enough to reach Darlene, Wesley was not unable to stop smiling, "Hey sissy, hold me sissy" while Lesley began kissing her cheek, saying "Me too, me too.

Both boys were wanting to climb on the bed and hug her so Rolf held them saying, "Hug her gently" so they did what daddy said and hugged her gently. Finally everyone said their good-byes as Victoria, Ralph and Rachel left with the boys (Wesley and Lesley). They were waving and saying, "Bye, bye sissy, bye, bye mommy bye, bye daddy" not understanding that this was their last good-bye to their sister.

Afterwards Rolf walked back into Darlene's room, she turned to him and said, "Daddy I love you" then she added, "Daddy I do not think I am going to live much longer" he burst into tears. Darlene reached out her hand saying, "Daddy everything will be alright because that means I can go to heaven so please don't cry."

Rolf was speechless for a moment then "Please don't leave baby I just do not think I could bear loosing you." She looked up and smiled at him as she said, "I am sorry Daddy please try to understand I just don't think I can stay here with all of this pain and I think God is ready for me now." Her little hand still held his.

Rolf turned as he felt a hand touch his shoulder it was Isabelle. Looking at her Darlene said, "Mommy I have to do something before I go to heaven" fighting back the tears Isabelle said, "What is it my darling" with tears swelling up and her heart breaking. Darlene said, "I heard the nurses talking about the drunken man that hit us is in jail."

Rolf shouted, "That is right he was drunk" Darlene replied softly, "Please get the police to bring him to me so I can forgive him." Isabelle said, "Darling, you can forgive him without him being here." "NO because I could not forgive him for taking away my family he needs to die" shouted Rolf.

Darlene said, "Daddy please don't let this take away your heart God loves us all." Remembering what he had done (killing his father and as a result taking away a member of the family) Rolf softly whispered, "Baby you have more wisdom in your young mind than many people that are well educated and much older."

Darlene whispered, "Please let me rest for awhile then I will speak to the drunk driver that hit us alright." Fighting back the tears they kissed her and walked out into the hall. Isabelle said, "Rolf you have to set aside your feeling and let her have her last request" looking at him with a look (I mean what I am saying.)

Knowing this in his heart, Rolf went to the police department to try to bring the drunk driver back to see Darlene. He walked into the police department and asked an officer behind the desk, "May I speak to the Captain in charge." The officer asked, "Sir, what is this about?" Rolf looked seriously at him, angrily shouting, "It is about our accident with the drunk driver that injured my children."

The Captain overheard the shouting and came out of his office and said, "Mr. Chamberlain, will you step into my office." Rolf asks, "How did you know my name?" as he followed him. The Captain replied, "This is a small town and everyone in town knows what happened to you and your family. I am so sorry about your children especially your little girl."

Rolf said, "That is why I am here" "Sorry I don't understand. We have the one that caused the accident" said the Captain. Rolf said, "Yes I know however I have a dilemma. My daughter is dying from her head injury, she received from the accident caused by the drunk driver you have in your jail."

Holding back the tears, Rolf whimpered, "However that is not my dilemma" The Captain looking confused and scratching his head asks, "Just what is your dilemma, Mr. Chamberlain?" Rolf said, "My daughter is only nine years old and she wants to speak to the drunk driver that hit us, so she can forgive him face to face."

The Captain stood up, as he stated, "You know Mr. Chamberlain, this is a highly unusual request." Rolf said, "Yes, I know however, my daughter is an unusual nine years old. This is her last request and we HAVE to honor it," looking ever so serious at him. The captain replied, "If I remember right, the last encounter you had with him, you wanted him dead; Am I right?" staring back at him ever so serious.

"Yes, you are right however, I have to focus on my daughter's last wish, not my own feelings right now. Could we please make this happen for her sake" said, Rolf as he stood up, adding "As you are aware my daughter has only a short time to live, so please take this request seriously." The captain said, "Let it not be said, that I stopped a dying child from having her last request met. Let's go" as he led the way to the jail cell, to release the prisoner.

Finally, they arrived back at the hospital, Rolf turned to the prisoner and said, "My child is dying, so watch your words," as he raised his left eye brow. The captain, the prisoner and Rolf walked into Darlene's room. Isabelle looked at Rolf, saying, "She is getting weaker and the time is short She still wants to talk to the driver."

The Captain approached the side of the bed with the prisoner and said, "I am Captain Leonard and this man is the one that hit you, his name is Curtis Tillman." Darlene looked at the driver and her voice was weak, she softly said, "I thank God that he let me live long enough to see you, before I go to heaven."

Curtis took a deep breath and said, "I am so sorry that I hit you." He held his hands over his face and cried uncontrollably, as reality hit him, of the seriousness of the accident and knowing it was his fault for drinking and driving. Everyone in the room was wiping tears away from their eyes.

Darlene took his hand, saying, "I know you are sorry, I can tell you are and I forgive you, before I go to heaven." Curtis whimpered, "No, you are not going to die, you will be alright" looking over at Isabelle shaking her head, fighting tears he realized it was true, she was dying. He cried uncontrollably again.

Rolf said, "I think she has had enough and she has forgiven you, so it is time for you to go" Darlene looking at Rolf said, "Daddy, wait I am not through talking to him, please" so he backed up. She was looking at Curtis, as she said, "Yes, I am dying but it is alright, because I am going to heaven to be with God.

Curtis was still crying, as he said, "What can I do for you?" She said, "You can tell other people how much God loves them, as he loves you." Shocked, He asks, "God loves me?" "Yes, he does and that is why he brought you, to me, so I could tell you." Darlene asked, "Will you pray with me?" He said, "Yes" She said, "Repeat after me, Oh God Please forgive me, of my sins and come into my heart, amen" he smiled, as he knew that God had forgiven him at that very moment.

After Darlene prayed the prayer of repentance with him and he said, "I promise, I will tell others about God" and at that moment Darlene's hand dropped from his and she drew her last breath and died. Isabelle began to scream and cry hysterically. Rolf took Darlene in his arms, held her tight and cried loudly "Why GOD, Why?"

The Captain grabbed Curtis by the arm and rushed him out of the room. The doctor and nurses came rushing into the room to help. Sadness filled the room, because this little girl (Darlene) had touched them all, so tears were coming down the cheeks of each and everyone in the room.

Later, after Darlene was taken away, Rolf and Isabelle left the hospital and checked into a hotel to rest and make decisions for her funeral. Rolf called Ralph crying, "Ralph my baby in dead and I am sadder than I have ever been in my life" Ralph replied, "I know, I wished I could take your pain away."

Ralph continued, "Would you like to bring her to Atlanta, to bury her in our family plot?" Quickly, Rolf said, "Yes, I would like that, but let me talk it over with Isabelle first" Ralph said, "Let me know your decision, when you know" and they hung up the phone. Isabelle lay across the bed, too exhausted and overwhelmed to talk at that time.

Rolf lay across the bed with her and held her in his arms, for much needed quiet time and rest. They fell asleep. Later, when Rolf wakes up he ordered room service, for food. After Isabelle wakes up, they eat and he asks, "Isabelle my brother Ralph said, if we would like, we could bring Darlene to Atlanta, to be buried in our family plot, is that alright with you?"

Isabelle said, "I think that would be a good thing, I think Darlene would like that" so Rolf called Ralph back and the arrangements where made. The day of the funeral Rolf stood up in the church and said,

"Darlene was only a nine year old child, but she was sent here on this earth for a reason. She was like an angel that swept over and captured our hearts and led us to God our heavenly father, showing us his love."

He continued, "And with HIS love, he could lead us the way to our heavenly home, where our little angel Darlene, that he loaned us for awhile has gone and we will always, love and miss her; thank God, he let us know her for a while, Thank-You God, Thank-You.........

They buried her in the family plot and put a statue of an angel of her size on the grave to let everyone know that this little child was most like an angel they had ever known.

THE END